Clean Sweep

Clean Sweep

JEFFREY WALLMANN

BARRIE & JENKINS

COMMUNICA-EUROPA; LONDON

Men blush less for their crimes than for their weaknesses and their vanity.

– La Bruyère, *Characters*

Chapter One

'Merde,' Kalenberg said.

René Serault glanced from his deck chair, squinting, the July sun a mid-morning ingot. Towards Kalenberg who was leaning against the balcony railing, a gargoyle on the face of Notre Dame. 'Dieter, I do believe your French is improving.'

'I had lessons last night I'm not about to forget. Not that I'll have the chance to before my trial. Where's that drink you promised me on the way here?'

'We've only been here ten minutes. Jennica will be out with the wine, but give her a chance to get dressed.'

'How long can she spend putting on a bathing suit?'

'Like making love, the less there is the longer it takes.'

'Love. The last time I was here, the girl was called Lillie.'

'Ah well, a slight rotation of crops.'

'Wretched how you treat women, wretched.'

'Hypocrite. It's well known your electronic service is only a ruse to board yachts and ravish girls. Grand old satyr of Menton harbour, repair kit under one arm, pants draped over the other.'

'Absolute slander. You should be ashamed.'

'I wish there were something to be ashamed about, Dieter. Or lustful about or hopeful about either. There isn't. I'm dead tired, the desire's all burned out of me.'

'Balls.'

Serault sighing a weary sigh, fumbling beneath his chair for that morning's copy of the *Nice-Matin*. Unfolding it; stretching out lean and angular; his face oddly asymmetrical

7

and etched with lines. Especially at the corners of his deep-set walnut eyes and between his straight nose and thin tight mouth. A miniscule white scar ran across his neck, and his voice had a smooth huskiness to it because of the resultant thickening of his vocal cords.

Kalenberg turning to look at him with exasperation. At the bony fingers and striped shirt cuffs, the casual beige slacks and suede loafers – protrusions from around the butterflied paper. Where Serault's head should have been was a front-page photo of a demolished Renault and the caption: FAMILY KILLED ON WAY TO BE BLESSED.

Kalenberg asked: 'Anything on the inside?'

'Monégasque Red Cross Gala.' Serault cleared his throat. ' "The most important charity ball for the Côte d'Azur and Riviera dei Fiori will take place two weeks hence, Friday, August the Third. In a marvellous décor of cretonne and tulle fishnet, the romantic theme of Neptune and his under-water kingdom will lay host to Society the world over. Music will be provided by André Rasseaux and his dreamy violins, and drawings for the extravagant lottery will include an album of stamps donated by the Prince, a shawl of swakara, a gallon of whisky, a litre of perfume, a – " '

'I meant about what happened to me.'

'Not newsworthy. Things like that are never reported.'

'I've been insulted and persecuted, and it's unimportant?'

'Unprintable. With a casino desecrated in gilded cherubs and ladies smoking cigars, Monte Carlo doesn't need any more vulgar publicity. You must face reality with the proper perspective.'

'René, you've never had your wallet stolen right after losing most of its contents gambling. You've yet to discover yourself penniless when presented with the dinner cheque.'

'I've yet to kick the Café de Paris manager in the shins.'

'He refused to believe I was a gentleman of honour.'

Kalenberg turned his back to Serault, resting his belly against the railing. Staring moodily at the view, filtered though it was through a haze of dust and debris. A broody lull broken only by the dump trucks and scoop-shovels a hundred feet below the balcony, noisily excavating holes in the brown puddingstone cliff.

Serault's house perched on a small knoll at the right edge of Roquebrune, a medieval village of great charm and inconvenience hewn from the battlements of a tenth-century Carolingian castle. A few of the village's red pantiled roofs could be seen, a cubist canvas of haphazard angles, but the main rookery of tangled alleys and knee-breaking stairs was just out of sight. And, conversely, the balcony was private. Behind rose the southern edge of the Alps, dour and spare; beyond the excavation, a hillside terraced with white villas dropped steeply to the Mediterranean. Dark cypress, olive, pine, and aleppo speared the furnace sky; aloe, Lentisk, and pink ficoids clinging to garden walls slumbered in drought. The sea was a blue steambath; the beach hard pebbles; the coastline a crescent from Monaco five miles to the right, to Cap-Martin diagonally to the left – an exclusive promontory hiding Menton and the scurfy Italian border from sight.

Serault refolded the paper and regarded Kalenberg, who was squat and beefy inside a suit the texture and design of upholstery fabric, his tie like a hemp-rope noose. His eyes bloodshot, his jowls unshaven – not unnatural results of having lodged overnight with Monaco's Sûreté Publique – and his fringe of greying hair was covered by a pith helmet of the platter type usually worn by Congolese missionaries. They'd been speaking English because what little French Kalenberg knew was incoherent behind a guttural accent. This lack was an affront to Serault. Now, running his fingers reflectively over his old knife scar, Serault decided Kalenberg was an insult to all Gallic sensibilities.

'Something in the German character,' he said at last. 'A distinct undercurrent of frenzy to it. You're an excitable race.'

'So're your police. Arresting me, holding me overnight. A small dream I had, to repair marine electronic gear. A dream wrecked, the last of my savings torpedoed at the tables and shanghied by thieves. And because I was a bit indignant, I

9

now face pawning my equipment to pay some no doubt exorbitant fine.'

'Calm, Dieter, keep calm.'

'I am calm. I've nothing left to keep except my calm. And you, you indigent bastard, the police refused to take your cheque.'

'Unfortunately they'd heard a rumour that my inheritance has been devoured by poor speculations.'

'Women and schnapps.'

'Such bitterness. And after I drove to Monaco to bail out you and your car. And post this very house as security.'

'They almost didn't accept it, either. Your walls are papered in mortgages and notes, and finally I had to co-sign my own business to make up the difference and get released.'

'The gesture is what counts.'

'Your gesture will worry you until I show up in court.'

'Ah well, I can't deny I'd hate to lose my poor home. It's all I've left now, my final resting place.'

'Now you make Roquebrune sound like an elephants' graveyard. Look at this view. René, it overwhelms even you.'

'The villagers all lie and cheat, and their dogs are legion. I must walk with head bowed for fear of stepping wrong.'

'I'm finished, kaput, and you bleat about lolling in the sun.'

'Please, lower your voice. My hair hurts this morning.'

'It should,' the girl said. She was walking out from the living room, bearing a wicker tray with glasses and a litre of chilled white wine. 'The way you drank last night . . .'

'Merely testing various vintages, chérie.'

Kalenberg swivelling around, commendably agile for his bulk, Serault introducing him to Jennica Fey. She was perhaps twenty-four, sensuous but not overly beautiful, though her breasts were good. She moved lithely, barefoot, thighs jutting. Her blonde hair swept in two curving wings from her forehead past her ears to knot loosely at the nape of her neck, framing an oval face of wide-set eyes, delicate nose, and plump mouth. She wore neither make-up nor lipstick, accentuating her schoolgirl illusion.

10

The look she gave Serault was distinctly older. 'Various vintages? None over six hours old and all with the same label.' Her accent was South Kensington, the British equivalent of Serault's Parisian birthplace, the 8th Arrondissement. 'Does he always fib so shamelessly, Mr Kalenberg?'

'Call me Dieter, and yes, often worse.'

'Vipers, the both of you. To my bosom. One freshly sprung from jail, and the other an itinerant veil dancer.'

Jennica slammed down the tray. '*I* am an actress.'

Kalenberg watched her prance stiffly back into the house. 'A nice one she seems, René. Better than you deserve.'

'Christ, I need this.' Serault pouring wine into the glasses. 'Stop worshipping craven images, Bernard, you don't know the facts.'

'What've you done?'

'So happens there's been a slight disagreement, nothing serious but going on a few hours now and becoming wearisome. Happens between the best of couples. Oops! The terrace just moved.'

Kalenberg glanced warily over the railing, at a concrete-mixer pouring out a temporary retaining wall. 'From your excavation?'

'Not mine. It's the SBM's doing, and I do believe the day will come when this entire house will sink into their pit.'

'SBM?'

'Société des Bains de Mer – Society of the Baths of the Sea. The grandly misnamed cartel which runs the casino and most of the other tourist haunts in Monaco.'

Irascibly: 'That I know. But why are they digging here? They're not planning to build something in front of you, are they?'

'Not allowed to; some law about scenery being an endangered species. No, they're tearing down the old Summer Sporting Club at Larvotto beach, and constructing a new one on a landstrip there. They need fill, but the area being built up the way it is, the closest place for suitable rock was my property.'

'You have no honour.'

11

'I had no money when they made their offer, so I had no choice. At least this way something comes in once a month.'

Kalenberg surveying the rape below; then glancing farther along the hillside to the western boundary of Roquebrune – Cap-Martin, and beyond to the fashionable beach of Larvotto. Where a barren jetty was slowly growing out into the sea. 'That's it?' he asked, pointing. 'That finger in the water?'

'Thumb, friend, the omnipotent thumb.' Serault slouching lower in his deck chair, glowering. Able to see between the balusters to the distant landstrip, a cancer fed by the continual procession of Saviems, Berliots, and Fiats.

Where in a year would be trees and buildings and seagull tourists, there was now only packed earth, dull and flat and vaguely obscene against the backdrop of Monégasque glitter and glare. Farther along the shore stretched the rest of the Principality – cosmopolitan Monte Carlo, with its greenish bulbous-domed casino; Beausoleil, across the French line; La Condamine, the narrow business strip around the harbour; the palace of old Monaco-Ville on its peninsula; and, on its other side, the industrial suburb of Fontvielle, with brewery, power station, flour mill, and chocolate factory. A miniature kingdom half the size of Central Park. An anachronism crammed to the ramparts with the ancient and the modern, torn between mummified dukes pledged to the traditional and Levi-ed kittens swinging the slot machines.

A cultured and civilized jungle, Serault thought. Drained me for years and still is. The trucks remove my assets as inexorably as the croupiers did before. The monthly pittance from SBM is but a cruel hoax, a false buoy allowing me to drown gradually, instead of sink all at once, an impoverished stone. Come to think of it, it is as illegal to take the rocks as it is to build on it, yet this is only a minor annoyance. Nothing can stop them. The Orwellian vision. That boot. Directly in my face . . .

Kalenberg looked at Serault again, this time a bit solicitously. 'René, your argument. It wasn't because of me, I hope. I phoned so early . . .'

Serault shook his head. 'A poor second to Wesley Talmas.

12

Met him once, briefly last week, but he's American so he woke me up anyway. Matter of fact, met him the same night I did Jennica. Oh, and the garage also beat you: my car will be finished tomorrow.'

'But whose mini were you driving this morning?'

'Jennica's. My Citroën had its door torn off by a passing motorist – just flipped into the street like a biscuit. Ah well, no matter. It's the paper that started the trouble; Jennica reading about the gala. But God, tickets are 600 francs each. The more absurd the occasion the higher its cost. A whore's philosophy.'

'Rot.' Jennica returning, peeling an orange.

'I've lived here since I was five, and I tell you it's all done with mirrors, all sham and delusion.'

'It is glamorous and exciting,' she said. 'The prince and princess and everybody who's Anybody will be there, and I want to be too.'

'The annual joust of the social season. But Society has syphilis – '

'Oh, tell the truth. You're afraid to go because of Nicole.'

Kalenberg eyeing Serault slyly. 'Nicole?'

Serault uneasily: 'Nicole Hibou. Father made a fortune in vinyl purses. She lives out in Cap-Ferrat with them in an indecently large villa; four gardens, tennis courts, everything.'

Jennica leaning against the deck chair, flicking orange rind past Kalenberg and over the edge. 'If you could take *her* last year, you can take me now. And I won't want any of your diamond necklaces, either.'

Kalenberg began to grin. 'René, you've diamond necklaces?'

'Only one, a family heirloom I used as an engagement present.'

'I see. To hook a rich bride.' The grin seeping wider across Kalenberg's muffin face. 'The necklace as the dazzling bait.'

'Kept,' Jennica purred, 'after she broke the engagement.'

'It was her right. The bitch.'

Kalenberg opened his mouth to laugh, then shut it and took off his helmet. 'When I think . . . René, is it very valuable?'

13

'Its centre was a 15-carat emerald-cut top Cape.'

'Ach, the impertinence of her. You must get it back.'

'Certainly. However – ' Serault leaned forward, smiling affably as if unconcerned while ticking off the points with his fingers ' – she screams at the slightest provocation. Her father owns a horsewhip. A platoon of servants, thugs in liveries. Her weimaraner comes to my waist. The villa's safe is in the wine cellar, and the necklace is stored inside, never worn.'

'Yes it is,' Jennica said. 'Once a year to the Red Cross Gala.'

'Ah well. But remember you yourself said I was afraid to attend.' Serault sat back to rub fondly along her leg. 'Why, one glimpse of my necklace and I might do something unforgivably gauche.'

'I can see it now. A quick grab, then lost in the crowds.'

'Imbecile. Every fifth person in Monaco is a flic, and for galas more are hired. With the new sporting club unbuilt, this gala will be at the casino, which has its own security force. Their last robbery was years ago, and then not in the casino itself. A thief in the underground snatched Baroness Grono's ostrich bag.'

'Underground? Here?'

'Not like your London underground. This is an elaborate network of passages connecting the Hôtel de Paris with the casino and other buildings, to hasten rich pedestrians to the gaming tables. During the gala it is watched, and there are guards and plain-clothes detectives and occults – '

'How French,' Kalenberg cut in, jabbing with his helmet. 'Hiring palm-readers and crystal-gazers to predict crimes.'

'Your ignorance is charming, Dieter. Occults are casino agents known only by the director, who spy on everybody including the staff. And there are physiognomists on duty too, reputedly able to recognize people after twenty years' absence.'

Jennica said, 'I bet I could disguise you to fool them, if I wanted to. I bet. I've studied costuming and make-up.'

'Cordons of police, hundreds of waiters and guests. And

you are urging me to rip and run, dressed as a *petit jésus*. I'm shocked.'

'Hardly. You've thought about breaking into that villa. I know you have, and I dare say about the quid your necklace would fetch.'

'Why stop at just that, chérie? There'll be over 250 million francs' – or as such things are computed, upwards of 50 million dollars' – worth at the gala, what with one tiara and another.'

Jennica turned to Kalenberg who was fanning himself fitfully. 'You take me to the gala, Dieter. I'll help steal René's necklace and sell it, on condition we don't split a bloody cent with him.'

'See her feral gleam, Dieter, her pointed teeth.' Serault laughed once, sharply. 'The Monégasque prison has a sea view. It catches the breezes, and the jailor's wife is known for her cuisine.'

'Home,' Kalenberg said bleakly and clapped on his helmet. 'But in the meantime, René, could you spare a few centimes – '

'Money?'

'A small loan to tide me over. Must you force me to beg first?'

'I've been considering the profession myself.'

'It's impossible fate meant for us to meet. I haven't deserved it. Paper, you mercenary, I'll sign an IOU.'

'I don't want your IOU. I'm so hemmed in by obligations at this point, I can't remember what I was complaining about last year. But I think there's thirty francs in my jacket pocket, hanging inside.'

'Lebenstraum! René, forgive my words. You're truly a jewel.'

'Don't ever, Dieter, *ever* use that word around me . . .'

Serault sat watching Jennica lead Kalenberg from the terrace, in search of his jacket: Jennica supple with her model's glide, Kalenberg lumbering with helmet askew, all belly and eyes and rolling round shoulders. The heavy sun, the glass of wine resting in his lap . . . Serault dozing now, the wine giving no inspiration, merely dulling a sense of despondency. And for that alone he was grateful. It was charming to drift along streams of disconnected thought . . .

Something surfaced in his melancholy flow. Slowly, across his closed eyes swirled an image more primitive than reason: dear, lamented Nicole, but no longer the pristine beauty he recalled. She resembled a pole-axed cow, staring haggard and pleading at Serault. While in his fist was dangling that damn diamond necklace . . .

Ah, to rob Nicole . . . No, to pluck every one of those hens, to gut the entire gala . . . ! Alas, such speculation was pure fancy. The casino requires guns to be checked in the cloak-room with the coats and briefcases, and bombs in truffles lack a certain savoir vivre. Still, as idiotic as it was, the vision was delicious to relish.

Serault smiled blissfully . . .

Chapter Two

Rompi-Cuou : Provençal for breaking your ass.

Should name my house that, Serault thought while falling naked down the stairs. A small ceramic plaque would do nicely, mounted outside the front door of this diabolical rabbit-warren – Maison Rompi-Cuou.

At the top of the stairs was the bedroom where he had shed his clothes. It was more of an enlarged landing with a canopied double bed, muslin mosquito netting hooked at one side of the headboard, odd socks gathering beneath the bureau. At the bottom of the stairs, Serault waited a moment to catch his breath, straightening slowly, rearranging the big striped beach towel over his left arm, the way a waiter might his serviette.

Into the living room, long and narrow, ending in a series of French windows overlooking the terrace. Tumid with fin de siècle furniture, remnants from the sale of his family home in Monaco after the death of his widowed mother. Carved mahogany and scrolled oak, silk brocatelle and worsted fringe, faded but not shabby, which was more or less how Serault considered himself. The room depressing him, the furniture cloying – parents gone, big house gone, now the money was gone and only this ponderous mélange remained. Worth nothing but unwanted memories, reflecting his past without expressing his taste. Minus an escape hatch.

To the terrace, pausing in the doorway to look at Jennica. Who was lying naked on a towel: on her back, the knot of her hair undone, one arm bent across her eyes. Breasts taut with nipples soft and inverted, loins flaxen and sparse, De Gaulle's moustache bleached. So nonchalant, so ignorant of tempering fears. Truly the single grace note to this dismal house, and God bless her and keep her from disease, for I no longer have the kingdom or the power. Or the ability to escort her to the gala, or, for that matter, let her wear

my

diamond

necklace

Amen.

The feelings which had been agitating Serault suddenly became self-evident: nihilism, angst, and an urge to rob the gala. At first, his obsessions struck him merely as asinine. Then galling in their own right as he realized how much worry and energy he'd wasted to reconjour that morning's mirage. After a gestation worthy of an elephant, his subconscious had given birth to the same fantasy again. Best to disregard all of this ridiculous waffling...

Walking onto the terrace, the sun a slap in the face. Approaching Jennica with pangs of affliction, desiring comfort and succour. She lifted her arm, glanced up. 'Was that you I heard?'

'I tripped on the stairs.' Serault spreading the towel and sitting down. 'Caught my heel in this Armenian flying carpet.'

'You drank too much of your cheap plonk, you mean.'

'Chérie, I've had one bottle, and that was shared with Dieter this morning and you at lunchtime. And you know how I mellow on very little, what with my wee stomach and wizened genitals.'

Jennica rolled over with a long-suffering sigh, her face hidden under her hair as she stretched out prone on belly and breasts. And Serault reached for a squeeze bottle of suntan lotion that lay near her uptilted rump. A flatulant noise, an obscene squirt, and white goo riveted between her shoulder blades. A direct hit, she never knew what brought her down. The lithe young body shuddered reflexively.

'Oh but it's cold.'

'I'll rub it in.'

'Just watch where you're rubbing.'

'I am, I am.'

'You're leering. I hear it in your voice, you dirty old man.'

'Look in my heart, not in my lap.'

'I've lived with you a week, and you've the heart of a lecher.'

'Any man would, faced with your immodest nudism.'

'Modesty is for virgins.'

'Once it was for ladies.'

A sniff, its meaning elusive, for Jennica kept her head averted. Serault daubing on more lotion, and now a little finger-painting for therapy. Ah, you are right and I am old. Thirty-five is no longer midway in life, it is the tag end of an era. I am aware of avenging sensibility; you are not, your generation never learning how carnal is knowledge. It is what makes the decade between us an abyss and not a gap. What damns me to be a dirty old man.

And feeling lecherous about it, too.

'Stop that.'

'Nothing risqué, Jennica, merely showing you my affection.'

'You can show it better by taking me to the gala.'

'Not that again.'

'René, it's my one chance at every girl's dream.'

'No sense to it. Most felons are more interesting.'

'Then be a felon.'

'Don't inflict me with motives baser than your own.'

'I wasn't.'

'I believe you. I do believe if it meant your going to the gala, you'd really like me to steal back my necklace.'

'I'd love it.'

'. . . And if I stole *all* of them?'

'Even better.'

'I'd need your help.'

'Anything.' Her voice muffled and flippant. 'What?'

'Ah well, I don't know what. Running errands and driving

19

the getaway car. Using your feminine wiles. Nothing strenuous.'

'No violence.'

'No violence. Only subterfuge and pretence.'

Serault squeezing out the last of the lotion. Helping it travel over the small of her back and her buttocks. Some phrenology along her lower spine, perhaps, those ridges and hollows surely having some significance. I play them like piano keys. A talented girl, I read, savoury and skilful if a bit too avaricious. Make an excellent partner in crime. As self-reliant and cunning as a man, equally useful most of the time and more so on a few occasions: late-night tactical sessions, dancing and judo practice . . . ?

'Stop fiddling with my bum.'

'A slight massage, to improve circulation.'

'René . . .'

'You don't want to burn, do you?'

'René, I almost wish we'd try.' She turned towards him suddenly on her side, curling. 'At least it wouldn't be this drifting.'

'Drifting? You're on vacation from the stage and cinema.'

'My dramatic career has been spent in the unemployment line.'

'Why, you told me you just finished a film.'

'I lied. I'm sorry I lied, but it was all too humiliating. My agent gave me expense money and sent me to Avignon without telling me even the title of the picture. When I got there I found out it was to be called "Bitch Brigade", and I was to play a WAC who infiltrates Nazi headquarters and gives nine generals the clap.'

She sat up, pressing knees against breasts, legs together and sugar-plums chastely hidden. 'I've done bad things, but not on film. I quit location and met you my first night in Monte Carlo. The Sunny Riviera, a way to kill time. I couldn't go back to London, to that spastic agent and my dreary flat. Oh René, even while doing bad things, they've seemed pointless, even while enjoying them. But I'm not bad to want money, am I?'

'Perhaps it's even worse to have had it once and then lose it.'

'It's not. It can't be. It's like heartburn all the time.'

Serault leaned forward and enclosed Jennica in his arms. No glib words coming to mind, there being a nagging truth to her despair. For if hers were a pointless drift, then his was a complacent wallow, the admission adding a curious affinity, a subtle feeling of responsibility towards her. Subversion! There'd been no whispered treaties of mutual security with this avid vixen. And yet, better her shallow greed than another's grinding piety, a woman reformer, a morbid tyrant. Cult of the Earth-mother. I am too harsh; Jennica is not the grasping wanton she fears she is, or the cool independent she'd like to believe. She's not what she thinks.

None of us are, and thank heavens for that . . .

Serault cuddled the girl, kissing her hair. Feeling the breeze flow along the balcony, hearing it sigh with the sound of withered franc notes. Watching particles of grit waft up from the rowdy excavation below and settle across her naked back. Kernels of irritant brown pepper.

Un grand sabotage de la Bal de la Croix-Rouge Monégasque . . . He had no idea how the innumerable problems and incredible odds could be surmounted if at all, and his thoughts all seemed buried under layers of gelatin. But the challenge was perfect tonic for his ennui. To conceive such a robbery would take nerve, inspiration, meticulous detailing and daring.

In short, a man like himself.

21

Chapter Three

Morning in Roquebrune Village: bright air sensuous with
lavender. Birds squabbling among the pines. Croissants
piquant in the bakery window. Serault buying a bottle of
Pastis.

He left the tiny grocery on Rue de la Fontaine. Cradling
the bottle, resisting the impulse to pause and nip. Sensing
the gala still worming up through his mind, and that he
shouldn't numb his thoughts in case it was close to breaking
surface.

Turning down the worn stone stairs beside the one-
woman post office. The one woman sunning herself in the
entrance. Bonjour, Madame. Bonjour M'sieu. A sharp right
at the Church of Sainte-Margueriete, the curate standing out
front throwing a rock at the village slut's dog. By the
butcher's doorway, beaded curtain keeping out pesky flies
and keeping in gossipy widows. Bonjour, bonjour, bonjour,
mumbling and bowing, moving up Rue Grimaldi and past
the other grocery – larger and closer to home, but here
Serault's credit has died and been buried in a pauper's grave.
Thorny old women out front, pinching tomatoes the way
their horny old husbands do the girls. Now out from the
capillary alley and into the sunlit Place des Deux Frères.
The fortress keep looming overhead, under siege by the
Louvre's restoration department, defended by twelve-foot
thick walls, cannon embrasures, battlements, loopholes,
apathy, etcetera. Serault sifting through his pocket lint for
cigarette change. Into the bar La Grotte, the same bonjour

bonjour while buying a pack of Gauloises, a ritual worse than a Gregorian chant. Miss once and you're blacklisted from the bistro and chopped up by the ladies in the butcher's along with their cutlets.

Serault went through the Place and down Rue R. Poincaré, the only street in the town able to take cars. A few yards farther and the village cluster ended, stringing out in separate villas and gardens. On his right was the slender, unnamed driveway leading to his house. Jennica's mini was parked beside the front door. The door was in diamond shapes, stained olde dark, with wrought-iron hinges. The mini was in menopause, hand-painted turquoise and salmon with an oval GB sticker on the back. Jennica was in jeans and a chambray shirt, and was yawning behind the right-hand steering wheel.

He wedged in the other side and shut the door, careful with his bottle. 'I hurried, but there were customers ahead of me.'

She turned the key and the engine ground to fitful life. 'Lord, I don't begin breathing before eleven. Why can't this mechanic return your car and you take him back to his garage?'

'That's British logic, which isn't inferior, merely reversed from the normal. Like your driving on the left. Here if I want my car, I must go to it.'

The mini snapped forward. Down the hill towards Menton, passing a gang of shirtless workers admiring a hole in the road. Serault said, 'Chérie, for dinner tonight . . . Perhaps a Dorade?'

'Give me some money to buy one.'

'As soon as my SBM cheque arrives.'

'Now. You gave your fat friend thirty francs yesterday.'

'My last. Dieter needed it more than we do.'

'Who's we? Damned if I'll spend what little I've left on fish. Borrow from this Talmas chap when you see him today, why don't you?'

'I've considered it, but it may be difficult. I think he was trying to tell me something on the phone yesterday; though it was hard to say and he could've been trying to apologize.

Easiest way to quiet him was to agree to meet for lunch, and leave it at that.'

Into Menton, Avenue Carnot, the seafront quai running parallel one block over. Children blackface with chocolate and dragging tin buckets. Mothers waspish from too much sun, and fathers grouchy from too much family. The mini creeping. Serault prowling for wet bikinis and sandy pudendas. Jennica with her hands gnarled around the wheel.

'René, you can't be broke. You just bought that bottle.'

'On credit, I swear.'

'Then how on earth do you expect to pay for your car?'

'The Pastis. An agreement will be struck over a glass or so.'

'That has to be the shabbiest ever. Trying to get some poor mechanic drunk so you can weasel out of the bill.'

'Bernard Ledoux is an old and honoured friend. Besides, I'm hoping there will be more to the agreement, keeping yesterday in mind.'

A right turn on Avenue de Sospel. Awninged cafés and cream-coloured apartments. Tuberoses in windows, memoirs in bookstalls, sandals in racks. Jennica staring straight ahead, the traffic a fog, then abruptly looking at Serault. Her face expressing revelation, as if the dark meanings of life had been rendered clear. 'Yesterday . . . the gala . . . You're actually trying to plan how to do it.'

'I can't plan the impossible. My government does it for me.'

Doggedly: 'You're going to ask him to help think of ways.'

'So a few questions, maybe. I hear the answers and quit. We won't think of a way; we can't. There isn't any. Never mind.'

Out of Menton and up the Caral valley for a couple of kilometres. Left on a fork leading by the Monastère de l'Annonciade, the mini undulating higher along the corkscrew road, among rugged spurs of twisted olive, scrub-oak, and maquis. Serault ruminating, finally breaking silence to

24

say, 'This may take a while. Would you please phone the Hôtel de Paris and ask Wesley to wait?'

'All right. You will be home in time for supper, won't you?'

'Depends on when I find Dieter. Better forget about the fish.'

'Talmas, and Kalenberg too . . . René, you *do* have a plan.'

'No, just a few notions muddy and murky.'

Half way to the monastery, and they reached a plateau partially enclosed by bare limestone ridges. On one side of the road was a meadow of sparse herbage. On the other side was an automobile wrecking yard with precise rows of junkers barely visible over its tall, high, well-kept wooden fence. The jib of a crane canted high, a skeletal church spire with cable and three-clawed crab attached.

Jennica braked, pulling into a clearing of hard-baked earth at one side of the yard. Serault getting out and going around to her window, then glancing up at the two-storey building beside them. At the brown tiles and faded sign over the gaping barn door :

LEDOUX & FILS

REPARATION . CARROSSERIE . PEINTURE

'No fils, no daughters either,' Serault said. 'Bernard painted the sign before he was married, when he was still an optimist.'

'René? . . . you're serious, aren't you?'

'Jennica, it's only an idea.'

'It'll be bloody dangerous.'

'Afraid? Would you do it?'

'I . . . suppose. Yesterday I said so . . .' Staring up, and possibly due to her awkward angle, her eyes seemed queerly intense. Strained, almost pained with puzzlement. 'Why would the others?'

'Perhaps they wouldn't. For differing reasons if they would; we all cut our throats with separate knives . . .'

A plume of dust. Serault turning his back on it to walk into the garage, dim and richly cool. Cars lined along the

25

right in various states of repair, orderly and quiet, Ledoux not working among them. On the left a paint stall, a car masked for spraying. Plus an office, partitioned with windows and furnished with the usual rolltop desk, walnut cabinetry, and bare lamp dangling from the ceiling by its cord. At the desk was, as always, Madame Ledoux, a stout woman of uncertain years beneath whom many a chair had sunk without trace. She was, as always, wearing a black bombazine of size suitable for sumo wrestlers, and was, as always, knitting.

'Bonjour, Madame. Your husband, he is out in the yard?'

Her shrewd face nodded, needles clicking faster with nasty jabs, camel nose flared of nostril to indicate long-term disapproval. Serault quickly crossing to the open doors at the rear, stone floor echoing his steps. One should tiptoe past such landscapes; she has the awe-inspiring presence of a beached whale . . .

Serault under the sun again, shading his eyes. Strings of fanglike car bodies stretched sharp and delineated over the corduroy ground. Nearby his '69 Citroën station wagon squatted smugly plump, an ID Break Comfortable to be exact about the model, tea-rose pink of colour and gross of body and red plush of interior.

'Bernard?'

'René? Your monster is repaired and repainted. Be quiet.'

Serault moved in the direction of Ledoux's hushed voice, to the left and up a rutted aisle. Between the remains of two Renaults, Ledoux was stalking, crouched and with a jackhandle raised. Serault, closer, saw two large crows scuffling in the dirt as if to mate.

'Oyez!' Ledoux pounced, thrashing the handle. 'No filth in my yard,' and the Renaults were dented and the ground was thumped. 'Vice, lust, I won't tolerate it in my yard.' The feathered fornicators taking to raucous wing, handle sailing after them.

Ledoux straightened, a small pencil of a man with banjo eyes, a lounge-lizard moustache, and swarthy hair raked long for the modern effect, indignant in a checked suit of nipped waist and wide lapels. He smoothed his hand-painted tie along an ochre shirt. 'Too much of it on the globe as it is.'

'Bernard, your soul may be salvageable yet.'

'I have hopes.' Frowning: 'There's a hole in your trousers.'

'A small one, a cigarette burn I believe.'

'You wore those the last time here, and it's the same hole.'

'Same cigarette.'

'You wouldn't be such a barbarian if you spent half as much on clothes as you do on your car. What're you holding there?'

Extending the bottle. 'Man was not meant to thirst alone.'

'Sacrebleu! I hope Fifine didn't see you bring that.'

'I was careful. Quick, I feel dehydration setting in.'

Ledoux led the way as they darted between cars, veering towards the crane. Glancing furtively over their shoulders like one-eyed cats scavenging in garbage. The crane was formed from the chassis of a vintage Peugeot limousine – no doors, body cut off at the window line, jib rearing out of what had been the back seat and thrusting over the hood.

Ledoux reached among the levers and brought out two jelly glasses. He took them a few feet away, to a tap on the stem of a long pipe sticking straight out of the ground. Serault sat on the running board, wrestling with the bottle top. A cheery splash of Pastis in water, some shade and cameraderie on a summer day. Of such things is a person's weary lot made bearable.

'A toast to your derrick, Bernard. A welder's masterpiece.'

'A child can operate it.' Ledoux turned glum and made a wry face. 'There's a smell to this Pastis.'

'Naturally.'

'Unnaturally. It smells, René, of you not paying me.'

'Bernard, you can't conceive what I've been through lately.'

'I don't doubt. But something on account. Half, say.'

'My insurance agent is avoiding my claim. I've baited traps with blank policies, but so far he's evaded them with uncanny ease.'

'A third, I'll settle for a third now.'

'My bank sends overdrafts and the only bistro extending credit has turned into a watering trough for Lesbians. This month's payment for the rock is late, but I expect it shortly.'

Serault pouring a dollop more Pastis to sweeten things a little. 'A slight delay at best, Bernard. Nothing to concern yourself about, though I'd appreciate a kind word passed to your wife so she won't fret.'

'Fret.' Ledoux closed his eyes. 'You're ruining me.'

'Profit through clean sweat is a thing of the past, anyway. It's futile to dream of honest prosperity in this day and age, it's all gained through crime now, especially when done within the law. And I feel I must share a deep secret with you.'

'My heart won't stand it.'

Huddling together on the running board, the spirit of brotherhood wet and oppressed. 'Bernard, I'm on the verge of something.'

'Bankruptcy.'

'Ah well, that too. No, I've a wild idea. It hasn't developed yet, but I feel it deep down inside me, growing, fermenting.'

'Best ideas are that way. Sitting there awhile before bubbling up where you can see them. What's risen so far?'

'In strict confidence.'

'I'm a man of ears and no mouth.'

'. . . A robbery.'

'As a property owner, René, I warn you I consider robbery a despicable and heinous crime. Tell me more. A bank?'

'The Red Cross Gala.'

Ledoux was genuinely shocked. 'You're joking.'

'Originally I was, but since yesterday afternoon I've been gravely wondering how to pluck les grandes poulettes of their jewels. The few methods I've thought of are all unrealistic, yet it's taken hold of me I tell you, gnawing at my nerves, making sleep impossible – '

'– Dislocating your brain.'

'Still, I've the feeling that with a little effort and luck I can shape together a solution. I keep returning to one basic fact,

28

you see: I must use what's easily obtainable. I'm not a Corsican brigand or a Marseille chieftain with an underworld of experts and supplies. I must rely on what is openly and readily at hand.'

'And what besides insomnia have you got?'

'Jennica, an honest sinner. Very handy at art and crafts.'

'She's your current amoureuse?'

'Yes. Here, the bottle begs to be poured.'

Ledoux held out his glass with one hand, unfurling a handkerchief with the other and blowing his nose. 'René, if you do find an answer, I predict it will carry you along. And René, if you do find an answer, do me a favour.'

'What?'

'Carry me with you.'

'From here? Bernard, you're to be envied.'

'I am a driven man.'

'You're a respectable entrepreneur in a healthy atmosphere.'

'This healthy atmosphere plagues me with chronic sinusitus. Takes me about an hour each morning to clear out the mucus, by which time the day is shot and it hardly seems worth it. My business is not my own, my business is Fifine's. Who is in the midst of some second wind and insists on proving her virility.'

'Virility is a masculine fear.'

'It's my horror. I'm nailed nightly to the bed; tonics don't help and neither does God if I fail. The mere hint of sex sends me rabid as you yourself saw. I'd leave in a flash if given the chance.'

'But where would you go? To Paris? Ah, I can picture you, the Parisian fop, snapping cuffs and abandoning pregnant lovers.'

'No, Algeria.' Ledoux sighing nostalgically. 'Left a strange impression on me, the rich life piloting those old Chinook helicopters from Oran airbase. I'm positive my love of finery came from there, all that mess, that squalid mess.'

'Have some Pastis. Bernard, I never guessed any of this.'

'I'd even go along with the luxury of just giving up, but it isn't that simple. Life drags one with it. I'll continue miserably where I am, making money when possible and love when unavoidable, paying my taxes and instalments and probably the Vattiers too.'

'The Vattiers?'

'Marc and Henri, two rascal brothers from Sospel who work here twice a week. My wife's latest social project. They're out on parole, but I suspect she has other designs on them, poor devils. Jail's preferable. Speaking of robberies, they tried holding up Sospel's largest company, the Mugeut Goat Cheese Cooperative, for the payroll. I'm short on details, but I understand they planned well, wearing stocking masks and using some guns left over from the Nazi occupation. Their father had been a Communist in the Resistance, so naturally when weapons were smuggled in he'd cache what he could for the coming revolution. The Communists did that all the time.'

'Were notorious for it. Another drink?'

'Don't mind if I do. There was an unfortunate mixup in bags at the last moment, but in the confusion the brothers escaped. Weren't caught for months, even though they stayed right there in the village.'

'Ah, that is nerve. Did they escape with much?'

'In a sense. Fifty kilos of goat cheese.'

Serault glancing down at his glass, over to Ledoux and up to the crane, and back to Ledoux. Stroking gently his scar. After a short while he said, 'Bernard?'

'Yes.'

'Bernard, could we visit the Vattiers this afternoon?'

30

Chapter Four

A noon sun preening at the height of day.

Serault driving along the Basse Corniche. Hunched at the controls, muttering to himself, the coastal road an inching conga-line of German, Swiss and Italian cars. Villas shimmering in the dead white heat, molars capping grey jawbone hills. Air flowing sluggishly past his open window, a stifling aromatic tobacco of rose and carnation and the tour bus in front of him.

Reaching Pont St-Roman, the eastern border of Monaco. Turning off on Route du Beach, longer and trickier and almost as cluttered, but at least the traffic was French.

Along Avenue Princess Grace. Balustrades and granite walls dizzy with wisteria, Monte Carlo Beach behind and to his left. Ahead, the old Summer Sporting Club was being demolished, a free-form of twisted girders and crumbled pink stucco, artistically improving the original 1927 design. Also a length of rough construction fencing, behind which trucks were laying the foundation for the new club with Serault's strip-mined rock.

Serault viewed the fence with distaste: my status quo is sliding down the drain. The cheque spent before its arrival. But my alternatives are equally obnoxious – robbing the gala in a fit of hysteria, or marrying some rich widow . . .

Past the egg-carton Holiday Inn, where it was rumoured an employee could actually speak French.

Up Avenue des Spelugues, a main artery suffering from sclerosis of discotèques, and searched until he found a parking place, Monaco's favourite gamble offering the worst

31

possible odds. A walk to the Place du Casino then, through the gardens fronting the casino's long, bay-windowed north façade.

At the Place, cars were chasing their tailpipes around a circle of sweet william and geranium known as the Camembert. The Camembert was a dot to an exclamation mark called the Boulingrins – avenues of more manicured flowers, palms, and huge cacti, which gently sloped up to the Boulevard des Moulins and Beausoleil beyond. Directly across from the Cheese from the Boulingrins was the casino's main entrance, elaborate between twin Moorish towers and florid angels. To the right of the casino was the Café de Paris – souvenirs, snacks, slot machines; umbrella'd tables awash with Dubonnet and Pils 58; lemminglike tourists jostling one another in hope of rubbing against Beautiful People. To the left was Avenue de Monte-Carlo and the Hôtel de Paris, intact as a museum piece in the same 18th-century baroque as the casino.

Serault, leaving the kerb at the Café. Through the traffic to the other side, where Cartier had a jewellers in one corner of the Hôtel. From the Cartier shop to the Hôtel lobby, down along a barbered hedge protecting the luncheon terrace from the sidewalk riffraff.

A shout, familiar and distinctive above the babble. On the terrace, a waving arm bare and pink as broiled lobster, though whether from overexposure to sun or liquor Serault could not tell. More appeared at the hedge: silken tie and short-sleeved shirt worn flashy and tight like a pudgy coiffeur's. The face of an aged baby, with toothy smile, grey hair *en brosse*, and eyes hidden behind bomber-pilot sunglasses. A mild voice missing the usual nasal grate of most Americans.

'I've saved a table near the back. It's not the one I wanted and we're having to share.'

'Wesley T. *ca va*?'

'If that's French for how'm I doing, my haemorrhoids have attacked and I've caught cold from my room's air conditioner.'

32

'Jesus! I'm not even seated before you demonstrate yourself to be a hypochondriac and social leper. What's worse, you don't care.'

Serault was berating the shrubbery, Talmas having slipped suddenly from view. 'Lady,' Serault heard, 'if that dog has pissed in my shoe, I'll drop it in your soup tureen.'

Serault moved at a hasty clip to the end of the hedge and up the steps, entering the gymnasium-sized lobby. Front and centre was the equestrian statue of Louis XIV, its horse's knee rubbed raw by superstitious gamblers. To Serault's left was a small lift, which descended to the passageway connecting the casino; and the entrance to the American Bar, somewhat reminiscent of the *Titanic*. To his right, a grand piano shone like patent leather, and the Louis XV Room, a dining salon which opened out onto the luncheon terrace. Serault angled towards the Louis XV Room. A rudder-bosomed matron dragging a wet toy poodle, sailing for Serault through the shoals of tables. Serault veering away, continuing down the lobby.

Lined behind the equestrian statue were three glass cabinets. Inside them was an unusual collection of sculpturings from the Louis, Regency, and Empire periods, mostly representing various segments of female anatomy, and adorned with jewellery lavish with diamonds, rubies, sapphires and emeralds. Beside the first case was a large placard propped on an easel which read:

TRADITIONS OF BEAUTY
CLASSIC AND DISTINCTIVE PIECES OF JEWELLERY
ON PUBLIC DISPLAY THROUGH AUGUST THIRD
IN HONOUR OF
LA BAL DE LA CROIX-ROUGE MONEGASQUE
UNDER THE PATRONAGE OF
PRINCESS GRACE AND HER HUSBAND PRINCE RAINIER
SPONSORED BY
HORSTEN
PIERRES . BIJOUX . PIERRES DE COULEURS
GRAND MAGAZINE À L'HERMITAGE

33

A guard with years of fatigue etched on his face impassively watched the display from a nearby leather armchair. Porters scuttled about in search of cigarette butts, discreetly disturbing elderly guests nestled amid the fronds and blue velvet. A cross-coloured ceiling supported a Laocoön chandelier. Mirrored walls with wainscots of dark mahogany reflected men of business escorting wives of industry or girls of trade. A pride of families, a couple of jabberwocky adolescents, no children aloud. Across the back stretched a bank of two lifts; cashier's cage with a wall of safety-deposit drawers; reception and information desk; central stairs to a mezzanine shopping arcade; magazine counter in a right-hand nook; and a corridor extending along the rear of the Louis XV Room.

Serault went down the corridor; past the rest rooms and around the corner to Louis XV's other entrance. Opposite was the Empire Room, an ostentatious cavern of marble pillars whose diners were almost as old and riotous as the Gobelin fresco panelling its far wall. The Louis XV Room and terrace were crowded. He recognized some of the patrons, mostly local branches of family trees whose leaves were yellowing in the *Almanac de Gotha*. A few bent limbs: the yacht captain smuggling drugs from Tangiers; the Zermatt cardshark; the collegian-looking sisters specializing in fellatio. Simultaneously.

Talmas was wedged in a corner, next to a pastry cart swaybacked under weight of calories. Serault sat down facing him; between them slumped a dress blazing in sequins, a blue-rinsed thing in it resembling the stewed prunes she intermittently stirred. A waiter on his way to collect the cart was detained. Talmas ordering *œufs en gelée à la ratatouille*. Serault choosing the plat du jour and the cheapest Rosé, 'experience being that a palate for vintage is one that can cough up the price'.

Talmas began polishing his glasses with the tablecloth. 'René, it's great you could make it today. I've felt stupid all week.'

'Please, not on my account.'

'It was Rozaffy's doing. He swore you were eager to invest a half-million, and I guess I came on pretty strong when he introduced us. By the time I learned of my mistake, you'd left.'

'Ran is the word.'

'So this lunch is by way of an apology.'

'No need, Wesley. Maurice Rozaffy's been out to embarrass me ever since I convinced him a white-tie formal was to be a masquerade of fictional detectives. He was presented to Comtess d'Arôte dressed as a rabbit; creative of him, coming as Poe's Lapin, if you catch the reference. But you'd no way of knowing; it wasn't your fault. Maurice is subtle and nasty.'

'Well, we might have the last laugh yet. Remember my idea?'

'Must I?'

'Jesus, René, it's a money-maker. This is the heart of the perfume industry, and America's your big customer. But essences travel poorly, and it'd pay to ship by jet instead of by boat. That'd be me, Avocet Air Freight, and so I wouldn't deadhead from the States, I'd fly back here with the Top Forty.'

'The Top Forty what?'

'Records. Don't you listen to the radio?'

'Not if avoidable.'

'The best-sellers, albums and singles. They're pressed in Europe now with lousy fidelity, so the original discs should be hot-cake items. And they'd *have* to be flown – a tune older'n a month is golden, over a year is classic, and past that, it's due for revival. I figure by specializing, I'll be able to lower rates and contract for a maximum payload of 25 tons each way, three times weekly.'

'4,000 tons a year of stink and noise. The mind boggles.'

'I need financing for the 707, revisions for cargo handling, and the first month's expenses. I've a brand-new deal for it, René, and it won't cost a centime. Before you say no, hear me out.'

The waiter served with a flourish, then hovered expectantly. When Talmas didn't respond, Serault asked: 'What entrée do you want?'

'Nothing more, thank you. I'm on a strict diet.'

The waiter was dismissed, making sounds too low for Serault to hear. There was a minor diversion while the old lady left, awheeze like deflating bagpipes and then Serault said: 'I feared it was because you couldn't read the menu.'

'Those words I can pick out. Had to learn, to stay vegetarian.'

'Amazing. Due to ulcers?'

'I understand it's a remedy for piles and colds.'

'Wesley T., my advice is that you'd do better to learn proper French. You'd have known how to shut off your air conditioner.'

'A bellhop did once and opened a window. The noise of traffic could've woken the dead, and by the looks of some of the tourists, it has. Not a bad room, really; splendid view of the bird droppings on the casino roof. Incidentally, what's it like in there?'

'You've not been? You must if only once. It is de rigueur.' Serault gesturing towards the casino. 'Inside is a large entrance hall, the back of which is La Salle Garnier, the opera house where nearly anything cultural takes place. To the left is what's called The Kitchen, where peasants can ruin themselves; a Las Vegas salon with those sort of games, and then the expensive *salons privés*. Below them is the terrace where the Red Cross Gala will be held in two weeks, and a posh discotèque, the Black Jack Club.'

'Well, I dunno. I never was any good at gambling, and if I wanted night-clubbing, I could've stayed home in Dayton Ohio. René, if I don't raise the capital in a month to cover my options, I can kiss the entire shebang goodbye. Now listen. I've organized a Panamanian corporation and you can earn ten per cent on whatever stock you sell, and – '

'Me? You want me to peddle this *toilette de papier* of yours?'

'You've got contacts, and you know how to make them buy.'

36

'You hardly know me, Wesley.'

'I asked around; everyone agrees about you. I still think you can do it.'

'I'm flattered . . .' A pause, Serault debating if and how to introduce his own offer. Confiding in Ledoux had been the first crucial step, safe in itself yet the definitive crossing from fancy to fact. He thought – he *felt* – Talmas to be kindred, but Talmas was unfamiliar, untested . . . 'However, Wesley, I might know another way to raise your capital.'

'If you're asking, I'm interested.'

'More money than you'll need, in fact, and quicker.'

'You seducer, end my suspense.'

'Not here.'

'My room?'

'Let's walk around a bit. I could use the exercise.'

Talmas signing the luncheon chit, and then off the terrace, through the Louis XV Room and into the lobby. Where Serault slowed as they passed the Horsten display. 'You've looked at the exhibit?'

'Often enough to be arrested for loitering. The perfect air cargo, y'know. To hell with records and perfumes; jewels are the ultimate ratio of value to size and weight. What's it all worth?'

Serault shrugged as if unconcerned. 'Oh . . . fifteen million.'

'Francs?'

'Dollars. For example, that pair of sapphire earrings. Very famous, 80 carats, and I understand were appraised twenty years ago at $360,000. Only Horsten knows what they're worth today.'

Out of the Hôtel and standing on the steps, Talmas pointing across the Avenue to the side of the casino. To the ground-floor windows of Van Cleef & Arpels. 'I can see the place from my room, it and the bird-lime. What about in there?'

'Five million, possibly six.'

'Jesus . . .' A plaintive expression to Talmas, like the eyes of a tropical fish. Up the street beside the terrace hedge, coming to Cartier where he hesitated. 'Diamonds, amethysts, topazes. Platinum watches and rubied money clips. Don't it beat hell?'

'You're leaving smudges on the glass, Wesley.'

Around the corner and up Avenue des Beaux-Arts, a short block of shops beside the Hôtel. Opposite, a theatre and a Winter Sporting Club, now used for the SBM offices.

Talmas expansive with gesture. 'Art galleries and antique dealers. Leather marquetry and silver épargnes and Carrara marble statues. Culture. Civilization. In the very air. René, I came hoping Monte Carlo would be like the sets in all those old movies, and now that I see it, it looks even better.'

'Often I suspect it's nothing but an old film set.'

Moving to the end of the block. Which was perpendicular to busy Avenue Princess Alice, and faced the tiny, formal garden of Beaumarchais Square. The square fronted L'Hermitage, a smaller hotel opulent in Second Empire Creamcake style. 'The Horsten shop is in L'Hermitage,' Serault said. 'Right-hand corner, across from the central post office. In case you'd like to see more candied fruit.'

'Better, I'd like to hear your way of raising fast money.'

Serault flicked cigar ash, studying Talmas. Finally decided to back into the issue. 'Wesley, how far would you bend the law?'

'You ask that of a man known for his virtue and ethics.'

'Fine, we won't discuss it further.'

'Now let's not be hasty.'

'Then what tempts you? Give an example; a crazy one; a bad one.'

'Well . . . F'instance, not even a clerk was in Cartier when we looked just now. We could've dashed in, grabbed, and flown away.'

'Wesley, it's been tried. There're four Monégasque and nine French police corps, and the only three roads from here to Nice airport can be blocked in as many minutes. Moreover, Cartier wasn't empty and clerks are liabilities. Clerks panic, not alarms and cameras.'

'In my opinion, electronic systems are over-rated. You get

38

too dependent on them and lose initiative. But don't play foxy with me, René, you're leading up to your own f'instance. Spill it.'

Talmas with his nose bent like a weathervane, seeking the scent. While they strolled down Avenue Princess Grace, along the rear of the Hôtel's annex and a police substation. Serault aware he must risk being candid. Or as candid as was absolutely necessary . . . 'Did you know, Wesley, that fifty million dollars' worth of jewellery will be worn at the Red Cross Gala?'

'Impossible.'

'You dropped your cigar. A low estimate, actually. Some of those old dowagers are ambulatory chandeliers.'

'Fifty million . . . But René, if Cartier is impossible, how . . . ?'

'I'm not sure yet. Frankly, I'm not sure if it can be done at all. Normally the plan comes first, but I'm working in reverse, finding out what I can plan with. Like a chef raiding his pantry for leftovers, whipping something together out of what he's got handy.'

'I see.'

'I believe you do.'

'René, I'm honoured. But I don't think I want to be leftover.'

'Perhaps my simile was poor.'

'No, it's not that. It's that fundamentally to the core I'm a coward. My analyst tells me I shrink from post-natal aggression.'

'Wesley T. You are a victim of your own salesmanship.'

'I believe him, René. He yells at me.'

'You've sold yourself the delusion of being docile. Which is the snare of extortionate psychiatrists and the swoon of domineering women. But you're a man first and foremost, and man by nature is a predator. Beneath your civilized trappings and flab, your blood cries for adventure, your spirit craves rewards so opulent as to be abstractions themselves. There's a jungle beast in you, Wesley, and it savours a challenge too overwhelming to resist.'

39

'If I'm a salesman, René, you're the Heifetz of hucksterism.'

'You've allowed yourself to grow soft and compliant, and for your own health I insist you accept. Assuming I find a way.'

'Very well, since I'm cornered. I'm still afraid, but I'm now more terrified of being further inundated by your catarrh of manure. Also, because it's so consummately impossible a dream, I'll never have to face up to my fears.'

'I might think of something, you never can tell.' Serault glanced idly across Avenue d'Ostende, his eye caught momentarily by one of the city's Corps Urbain painting the kerb, his Vespa triwheel van parked where he'd begun the stripes some yards away. Serault turned back to Talmas, smiling softly. 'I might think of a way, Wesley, just to spite you. After all, there's many ways to skin a cat.'

'Yeah, but they're all based on the cat being dead . . .'

Chapter Five

A left turn at the intersection leading from Ledoux's garage, away from the tropical port of mid-summer Menton. Ascending the valley of Careï, the road a thin, curved ribbon of molten tar, sharp and perilous. Moving up through a country of brilliantine hills and shadowed pine forests, crystal streams flushing from the clefts, shepherds drowsing among their sheep.

Serault wore his usual slacks and shirt, a quagmire compared to Ledoux's lightweight hounds-tooth jacket, saffron shirt and scarf, and flared vanilla trousers. Ledoux gazing out of the Citroën window, querulous from heat and humidity.

'René, I've had second thoughts. I want out.'

'It *is* your out, Bernard, your chance once and for all. Ah well, since you were only whining this morning . . .'

'I meant every word. But there's such a thing as being too desperate.'

'I counted on a partner loyal, shrewd, and brave . . .' Serault sighing with sly regret. 'You know best, though. So does your wife. You should listen to her, she knows what's good for you.'

Ledoux shrank against the seat. 'There's that.'

'There's her, to be precise. Working with you, Bernard, building a nest, facing the future together . . .'

'I've changed my mind again. What do I have to do?'

'The immediate question isn't what you do, but what you have.'

'I haven't the yard, not while Fifine's roosting there.'

'It may not be needed, don't you see? If it is, why then we'll figure out how to nullify her. Also, you've a knowledge of the area second to none except perhaps my own, you're a trained veteran skilled with cars and helicopters, and you know the Vattiers.'

Ledoux peered at Serault. 'Do you think they'll join us?'

'We can hope. They've had, according to you, past experience.'

'Never again a virgin once the sheet is stained.'

'Not always true. Knew a lady once who on her wedding night tried hiding her previous sins by sprinkling iodine in the bed while her husband slept. Unfortunately she forgot that bleach in sheets turns iodine an embarrassing yellow. Still, there's a lesson.'

'Treachery, thy name could also be Vattier.'

'Exactly. What's good about them is what's bad about them, and we'll have to be cautious – the harm is in the noise one makes. Here's Sospel; where do I go?'

Ledoux gave orders to stay on this road and drive out of town. In an easterly direction, past placid old men in rush-bottomed chairs, and female beasts of burden hunched under kindling and jugs. Through pine and scrub, beside terraced stone walls, between rows of vines and olive trees, among peasants using mule and wooden plough. The lane unravelled not by kilometres, but by centuries.

'The Vattiers have a small farm out here somewhere,' Ledoux explained. 'With a sister, I think. I'm unsure; only been up here once . . . Yes, there's their driveway. Careful, it's bumpy.'

Off the road, onto a washboard rut rambling through a *garrique* of thistle, kermes oak, and bare limestone. A waste-land field broken only by an oasis of fir and olive, towards which they were more or less driving, car tipsy and lurching, stones a rataplan against its underbelly. Once among the trees, the trail coiled like a lazy garden snake, then wandered across a weedy clearing to end in a bald spot beside a cabin. The cabin was of stone, lichen in the cracks and gorse on the

42

roof, windows shuttered to keep out the flies. Goats foraged close to the outhouse, a short leap from the rear stoop. A rusty Simca was parked in the bald spot, facing a long wooden porch. Closer now, and Serault could smell the region's heritage – Piedmont cookery of anchovies and garlic, *leteme* cigars, old socks. An indestructible scene.

Almost to the porch when the front door opened. Out onto the porch loped three *mëtis* hounds, gangly and flop-eared, yelping and snarling as they bowled down to the yard and in front of the Citroën. Behind the pack came running a lithe girl, wearing a cheap muslin slip cut high on the knees, laundry-boiled over the years to the opacity of lace gauze. Serault craned his neck, foot thumping distractedly for the brake.

'René! Watch out!'

'I am, aren't you?'

Ledoux now seeing the girl. 'Christ! They said they had a sister, but I thought . . . I assumed perhaps she was twelve or so.'

'Eighteen to the day, Bernard.' Serault computing: a mane of ebon hair, sloe velvet eyes, an anvil for a chin and a bit thick of haunch. Ah well, but an undeniable vitality to her as she blundered off the porch among the dogs and pattered barefoot past the car.

Two men behind her, the porch trembling beneath their boots. The first was short and broad, looked slightly like Kalenberg in girth, which was to say like Buddha. Bib overalls, no shirt, black curly hair all over his body, and a pyramid of a nose slanting parallel to his forehead. 'Marc Vattier,' Ledoux said bewildered, as the man charged by. 'And here comes Henri.'

Henri showing strong resemblance, a possible twenty-two to his brother's twenty-seven or eight. Leaner and longer, face pockmarked and tanned like pigskin luggage. No shirt either, but he wore a blue stocking cap, a windsock streaming behind his head. As he tripped headlong over one of the hounds. The dog licked Henri's face. Marc and the girl went around the side of the house, and now Henri plunged after

43

them, cursing with the guttural Italian patois of his Sespelene French.

A half-smothered cry, the sound of bleating, a splintering noise. Confrontation with the outhouse. The sister came doubling back into view, followed by stampeding goats, Marc, Henri, and the hounds. A lively sprint about the front yard, girl eluding brothers, brothers dodging animals, yet all intertwined as if in some geometrically complex quadrille. Serault and Ledoux watching through the grimy windshield. 'Admire her spirit, Bernard. Her tenacity, her ardour and fire. Most seductive.'

'René, René, what's happening?'

'Obviously a slight misunderstanding between siblings, no need to whimper.' Serault glancing with aroused alarm at Ledoux; he had a fevered look, the look of breathless paranoia. 'Bernard ... ?'

'Oyez!'

Ledoux leaping from the car, a snappy trot towards the girl, on tangential course to the others still pursuing. Serault clambering after, thinking fearsomely of crows and jack handles and *Grand Dieux, nous sommes au jus*. Ledoux intercepting, a feint and parry until he seized her by the arm. The girl struggling gamely, a foot on his instep and an elbow to his ribs, mouth widening to scream. Nice teeth, Serault noticed, before Ledoux rashly clamped a hand over her face. She bit his palm. Ledoux let go, screaming. The menagerie swarming, hemming them in. Ledoux gently tilting. The girl standing winded but arrogant.

Marc, loudly: 'He's not the doctor, Ginette.'

And Henri: 'Bernard, are you hurt?'

And the girl: 'Let *him* see the doctor, not me.'

And Serault, poised to bolt, slowly began to breathe again.

'Merci, Bernard, that was quick thinking.' Marc clamped meaty fingers on Ledoux's shoulder. 'What brings you here, eh?'

Ledoux pressing his hand against his belly, managing a weak grin. 'Pleasure ... and business. Meet my good friend, René.'

The Vattiers regarded Serault accordingly, Marc saying, 'René, business or pleasure, let's get out of this infernal sun. Ginette, fetch a fresh pitcher to the porch. Vite!'

The girl went a few paces, turned to flick a thumbnail off the tip of her nose, then moved towards the cabin with leggy, impudent strides. The men trailed, Marc watching her saucy buttocks and shaking his head. 'We were expecting the doctor, and thought it was his car when we heard you. An affaire de la famille.'

'Affaire d'honneur.' Henri said. 'Ginette had a fight with a boy last night. While on the porch, alone with him.'

Ledoux was aghast. 'You mean she . . . ? You fear . . . ?'

'We pray.'

Onto the scruffy porch, shaded by a bowed, messy roof. Serault whispering to Ledoux: 'A motley pair, obviously. We must remember the moral of the sheets. Remember the sheets . . .'

It was less a porch than a spare room: rusted oil stove, kitchen table, three hard chairs, an aged and vaguely rancid olive cask, rakes, shovels, parts left after tinkering with things surely to be fixed tomorrow. Marc levering heavily into a chair. Henri hitching his leg over a corner of the table and motioning for Serault and Ledoux to take the other two chairs. Sighing tragically. 'If only our parents were still alive. As it is, the best chance of marrying her is if she'll compromise herself, but so far the cow has refused.'

'Maybe last night.' Marc rummaged in the table's one drawer, removing a pack of greasy playing cards. Dealing himself a hand of solitaire. 'But that's our trouble . . .'

Left unsaid: What's yours?

Sounds of creaking chair dowels, goats milling, dogs panting. Ledoux leaning backwards, a symbolic gesture, and Henri studiously vapid. Serault watched the cards being methodically laid out and he thought: So. It's to the essence now, between Marc and myself. How to open? Something besides bonjour, would you care to join in a crime. Ask for advice? Peugh, a cringing approach, pathetically unoriginal and baldly transparent. These are thieves and pallisons ready

45

to pry cashboxes with their grandmother's bones, no telling what hotels and brothels their towels come from. Must use greater finesse. Some sparkling repartee would go well about now, to impress lads . . .

Marc gazed at his cards. 'You're doing great so far, René.'

'. . . I wanted to ask your advice. An . . . opportunity has come along and possibly you know of some men who'd like to help.'

'Not offhand.'

'I was thinking in the neighbourhood of two. Who are hungry.'

Marc paused with the king of diamonds. 'Hungry for what?'

'Profits from a fast job.'

The face remained stoic but there was a whetting to the eye. 'If anybody asks, how fast is fast?'

'Lightning.'

Henri asked, 'Is this another holdup?'

Marc concentrated on moving the king to an empty row. Serault smiled delicately and said, 'And I understand a few older tools of the trade are still stored around this area.'

Marc glanced sharply at Ledoux.

Serault adding quickly: 'Ah, how Aunt Sophia used to bounce me on her knee and tell wondrous tales of the Resistance up here.'

'Your aunt has a moustache. On a fat lip liable to get fatter.'

Ledoux blanched. 'Sanctuary! Fifine! Fifine!'

Marc slammed the cards down. 'The trouble with you, Bernard, is that you have the supreme threat and know it.'

'I've the supreme reason to take this risk and know it.'

'Heh.' Marc picked up the deck. 'And the risk is for . . . ?'

Serault shook his head. 'My plans aren't complete.'

'When will they be?'

'When I know what's available.'

The front door suddenly opened, an interruptive clatter. Out strutted Ginette still in her slip, it being too hot and too late for anything more. Carrying a large dented pitcher and jangly cups of tin, the cups hooked by their handles around her fingers, a set of grotesque modern jewellery. Her brothers unconcerned, Henri intrigued with a dozing hound, and Marc engrossed in reviewing his cards.

'You don't fool me.' She set the pitcher and cups down, affecting the same insouciant stance she had in the yard, face the colour of early rhubarb from scorn and umbrage. 'I hear the silence.'

A dog yawned, wagging its tail to the tune of her voice.

'Trouble,' Ginette said. 'Whenever you start getting into trouble, first comes the silence when I'm around.'

Virtuous Marc, clasping clean hands. 'Merely contemplating.'

'Contemplating, is it. Contemplating how to steal something.'

'A tantrum,' Marc said. 'Just proves you do need the doctor. Time you were a wife anyway, preferably a well-thrashed one.'

'After you two, I never want to marry. Especially a man. But the Day's coming for you; *Père* Germay is right when he preaches the Atonement. You and Henri will be there surely as Papa is now, yes and the things you've stolen and the people you've stolen them from. Staring you in the face, Marc Vattier. Staring you in the face.'

Marc moved a jack on a queen to form a ménage à trois.

'Let them get their things on that Day, Ginette. Then will be time enough.'

Ginette making a persimmon face. One swift flounce and a slicing with her open hand. Henri ducked reflexively, abandoning the table, Marc leaned sideways to avoid her roundhouse slap. The crack of a chair rung. Marc listing suddenly, a woeful cry while pitching backwards. Legs hooked ungainly beneath the table. Henri snatching the pitcher just in time. A blizzard of cards and a chaos of cups, the table descending upon Marc's defenceless belly. A thunderclap of passing wind. Hounds yammering in bandy-legged rout, Ledoux taking out his handkerchief, Henri in a soft-shoe of angry fits and starts, unable to decide what to

47

do with the pitcher. Rampant discord by all concerned. Except Serault, remaining calm and detached, examining earth, sky, shoes, tender breasts visibly heaving in a skimpy slip. Follow the bouncing black dots. Oh me oh my.

'And when that doctor arrives, he can keep his paws to himself.' Ginette's voice astringent as she pranced to the front door. 'Let him pass his diseases on to his own daughter – I don't want them.'

Bernard righting the table. Henri handing out cups of warm white froth. 'Goat's milk fresh from the pap. Very nourishing.' Serault placing his cup aside: 'Nice something can be said for it.'

Marc on his hands and knees now, collecting scattered cards and putting them on the table. 'Perhaps we should all lay down our hands, René. At least a hint. Don't you trust us?'

No further than queers wanting the soap picked up in a shower, Serault thought, saying: 'If I didn't, would I ask you to join?'

'Join what? Join taking risks, is all I've heard so far.'

'Risks?' Serault postured indignant. 'Bernard risked bringing me here. I risked asking you. Neither the preparations nor the job itself will proceed until we're satisfied with our safety. Your risk is a simple yes or no, and if yes, then what precisely is in your father's cache. Risks? You're not taking any risks.'

Marc belched, covering it politely with a fistful of cards. 'Then let's put it this way: There'll be risks, there always are, and the only way to judge risks are when balanced against rewards.'

'Ah well. Millions.'

'Millions plural?'

'To be shared equally after expenses.'

'Good god!' Marc glanced at Ledoux, who nodded emphatically. To Henri, sitting on the table again, blinking a lot. Thence back to Serault. '. . . But of course, Henri and I would count as two shares.'

'Now wait, my charity to the Vattiers orphanage is – '

'*Plus* the cost of our equipment.'

'What cost? It was all stol – given to your father.'

'*Not* that his sons would ever dream of violating their parole.'

Serault strangling on an impulsive bon mot regarding Vattier heritage, finally agreeing. 'But sisters and goats fend for themselves.'

Henri swung a worried leg. 'Marc, do you think – '

'Brother, I know. This is a poor region, depressed by taxes and inflation, and I'm feeling distinctly underprivileged. Yet don't you be a part if you don't want. You make up your own mind.'

Henri brooding . . . Removing his stocking cap, that peasant cap which traditionally is moulded to show various tempers such as love, hate, war, birth . . . Slowly rolling the stocking up to form a flat crown, signifying démarche, a line of action.

'Bien.' A plump grin on Marc, a satisfied kick at the wreckage of his chair. 'Then, Henri, do the honour of the olives.'

Henri put on his cap, a snug fit now, going to the decrepit cask at the near end of the porch. It was the common 300-litre tub, barrel-staved and strapped by two rusty bonds, pungent when he lifted its lid, and brimming with black wrinkled olives. Henri scooping out a handful, eating while loosening the cask's top band. While Marc continued talking:

'Papa fought in the FTP – Francs Tireurs Populaires – always maintaining the Official Resistance Army was more rightest than Mussolini. He died of apoplexy, January of '59, the day after De Gaulle was elected president. Mama's been gone for three years now.'

Henri had the band off and was pushing against the upper third of the cask. With an innersanctum creak, it pivoted aside like the tray of an eccentric lazy-susan.

Serault said, 'I'd never have guessed.'

'If only Fifine had a bottom,' Ledoux sighed, 'half so false.'

Henri reached down inside the shortened cask, bringing out oilcloth parcels. Disclosing six FN Browning 9mm automatics, two Sten guns still in cosmoline, and four 5-kilo bricks of RDX explosive, grey and smelling like marzipan.

Serault asked. 'That plastique, is it good?'

The brothers shrugged. Ledoux said: 'Probably. It ages well and loses little potency, which is more than I'm able to admit.'

'How do you detonate it?'

'A small bang to make a large bang,' Ledoux answered Serault. 'Most anything will work. In Algeria, we used fulminate of mercury caps or even little trails of powder we'd light by a match.'

'There's some Cordtex fuse down there, also some time-fuse pencils,' Henri said, with head in tub. Next came two regulation army canisters packed with ammunition. Five signal flares. A biscuit tin of 'fireflics', small cylinders that when dropped in gas tanks would fire the gasoline after a few hours. But which were questionable now, their rubber retaining rings having deteriorated. Two other, larger tins filled with four-pronged spikes resembling those metal pieces used in playing jackstones, and guaranteed traffic-stoppers when strewn on roads.

'That's it.'

Serault glanced from Henri to the pile, glum with gathering despair. The meagreness burlesquing his attempts, their obsolescence mocking any hope of contriving a workable scheme. 'That *all*?'

Marc, offended: 'You think we're a sheikdom with oil and foreign aid?' Then mollifying: 'Eh, we've also a lost-and-found department under the porch. A small but varied selection of wallets, identity cards, and odd papers that should pass most cursory checks. No passports, unfortunately. People don't carry them when shopping.'

Serault despondent, filing Marc's information without replying. What a disgusting mess, just when he'd exposed himself and his motives.

And yet, upon closer examination ...

Serault reviving with exasperation. Realizing abruptly he'd held clues to one of his problems since his luncheon with

Talmas, but remained blind to their significance until piqued by this rubble of war relics. Facing Marc and smiling now, wrinkles like fingers stretching his eyes, asking: 'Two questions. One, I've an associate who doesn't know French; can either or both of you speak English?'

Marc, in English, 'A little, if said slowly in simple séances.'

'Good. And two, do you think you could steal a tar wagon . . . ?'

51

Chapter Six

A half-moon smoothed Menton to a uniform umber, shadowing the narrow lanes with mediocrity rather than menace. Serault made the rounds of native bistros, ending at the grubby *Embarcadère* along the quay; workmen squabbling over cards and *jeu de 421*. Or curing upon tall wood stools watching bicycle races on the television that was propped behind the bar. Sad Algerians around the coffeemaker. The crippled beggar from the market square sitting stoic at one table, his alto sax propped on the chair beside him. At another table in the back next to the gumball machine, Kalenberg stared with stupefaction.

Until Serault said: 'Can't you talk?'

'Extreme shock does that to me. You've shattered my evening and most of tomorrow with twenty minutes of uninterrupted blather. What you're asking is both illegal and immoral. I deplore it.'

'So do I. Are you with me?'

'Only your arrogance supersedes your insanity.'

'Dieter, I don't deny it.'

'Yet I confess I can't seem to manage my own career, so who am I to judge you? It's depressing to consider how quickly ethics waver when one foot is in the meat grinder.'

'Are you with me, Dieter, or aren't you?'

'Was there any doubt I would be?'

'Fine. I'll let you know when and where we'll all meet.'

'I feel responsible for this.' Kalenberg raised his hand, signalling the bartender. 'Yesterday morning on your terrace, like being in the bedroom at the moment of conception. I wish you to know though, I don't feel proud or satisfied about it, and I'd appreciate you helping me forget by buying a drink. The bill for which you'll undoubtedly send me later . . .'

Chapter Seven

When Serault returned home, Jennica was in bed, reading a book on costume design. 'Well? Did you find Dieter?'

Serault walked to the window, nodding. 'He's agreed.'

'You don't seem overjoyed.'

Serault gazed out as if absorbed how the night had altered his view. The bright blue and gold of day had transformed into violet and indigo, the hills on his right blending with the water far below in a dark textured marble. He turned away ...

The cabal was complete.

He'd have preferred a larger and better equipped membership, but he knew of no others combining the essential compost of knavery and need. If he could devise a plausible method at all, it would have to evolve round the talents now collected. He itched with strategies, his mind a rash of intrigue. He scratched while undressing, scratched when he slipped in beside Jennica, scratched as he lay there in his peaceful bedroom. He scratched for a scheme and grew increasingly restless when relief never came.

'Too much,' he said after some time. 'It's too much for you, four men, and a handful of antiques.'

'Then you're giving up?'

When he didn't answer, Jennica put her book aside. 'Very well, the gala is out.' Light in tone and manner, as if to draw the sting from his depression. 'A shame, but I suppose it's rather a pipe dream. Think of some other jewels I can have.'

Serault smiled, kissed her ear with his tongue. 'Come to think, I can offer two fine ones in the rough. Not diamonds, but they've been in the family since I was born.'

'Don't be lewd.'

'Who was first, chérie? Walking in on me the night we met.'

'You hadn't locked the door. I couldn't tell it was occupied.'

'And standing there asking if you could hold it for me.'

'Don't be insulting, either. I simply didn't want to break an ankle running, just because some drunk was in the loo first.'

'Lavabo.' His hands slid from her back and down her shoulders to her firm and elegant breasts. Their nipples swelled erect, ripely waiting to be plucked. 'In France, it's called a lavabo.'

'Lavabo, then. You don't care in this country anyway, you're the ones who build them mixed. Tinkling together. You never know what you'll find going to a discotèque here – or get because of it.'

'Kismet.'

'I was highly upset as it was and you took full advantage of it.'

'I gave you my moral support the rest of the night.'

'That wasn't a support, that was a crucifixion.'

Hands gliding lower along a trembling belly. The muscles of her thighs tightened, her body tensing, reaching for somethings just out of grasp. She pressed against him, a moulding of flesh.

'Lord, René . . . You're worse than a Chinese water torture.'

Serault touched her inscrutably. Ah, my hand is a comb, a five-fingered comb. Into the valley of life rides my five-fingered comb, parting your De Gaulle moustache and diving recklessly into the headquarters. The powerful rotations of your feminine tide; I'm sucked into your whirlpool without a fighting chance. Stop, please stop, René, you're driving me mad. I laugh, but it is a Pyrrhic laugh for other fingers search

55

down and she's now tightening around me. Is that all yours? If it isn't this bed isn't as private as I thought. Jennica curled her hand in his loins and pressured gently, her face in the crook of his neck.

Serault rolled Jennica on her back to draw them into their improper conclusion. Strike while the groin is hot. She arched, quivering and throbbing like a virgin being taken for the first time, except that she wasn't and so was infinitely better. Woman, you are liberated and must labour equally in this sordid work. You're crazy, you're crazy and so awfully obscene. She undulated up against him in slow, teasing rhythm, legs snaking around and her ankles locking against his calves to pull him tighter into her. Levering, I can see my own hands sweaty as they clench you. Kiss the panting mouth and palm the urgent breast. We devour each other. We devour lips and hearts and muscle and marrow; what is given is meant to be taken away. The apocalypse. Squeeze the breast ... Squeeze ...

Grâce à Dieu, she has killed me. Again.

Serault lay with his head nestled on her breasts, listening to her clockwork pulse unwind. His designs and frustrations slowly returning. Quietness gradually leaving him, to be replaced by irritation and then desolation and finally surrender. Jennica is right, the gala is out. Considered in vacuo, my ambition is absurd, too grandiose and unwieldy. Dying of thrombosis and gout from an obesity of desire. Ready to be wheeled, vestigial parts dropping along the way, to the morgue for burial and requiem.

Parts?

Zut! There's life in the patient yet. But I've got to operate reversely as I did when recruiting my men and material. Instead of fitting pieces together, I must separate the whole to form a solution, its enormity having blinded and intimidated my vision. Forest for the trees. Divide and conquer ...

He made copious notes: and more copious love.

Not necessarily in that order.

Chapter Eight

The first meeting of minds.

Gathered on Serault's terrace after having parked distantly and arrived separately, safe there as anywhere and possibly more so. On the tideless air the heady breath of cheese and wine and *Pan Bagnot* – sandwiches of raw onion, olive, tomato, and anchovie. The table of checkered cloth, napkins, silver, a large umbrella angled just so. Beside Serault, an urn chilling champagne – not of the best quality, but celebration was in order, if only with Spumanti.

The Vattiers resplendent in clean undershirts beneath their overalls. Eating the food as their goats would attack blankets, bracing themselves for the painful ordeal of not speaking French. Ledoux sweltering in light Donegal tweed, cheviot shirt and pink tie. Talmas in screaming plaid bermudas, legs by Steinway. Kalenberg anointing his head with Ambre Solaire, having forgotten his helmet, and furtively eyeing the unopened champagne with the subtlety of a Saint Bernard. Jennica attending after a morning of preparing, in blouse and Levis and deceptive charm. Her début as hostess, perfidiously domestic, seemingly happy doing what she should have been doing long before.

Talmas looked askance at his bowl of salad. 'Excuse me, Jennica. But I think there's meat in the dressing.'

Ledoux tasted. 'That's not meat, Wesley, that's ham.'

Talmas momentarily confounded, then: 'Isn't it uncomfortably hot today in your celluloid collar and spats?'

'A serious occasion requires impeccable attire.'

'Not quite,' Jennica said, picking up the salad. 'Your tie, Bernard, is Leander pink. British rowing club colour, you know.'

'I didn't, and being French don't care. Yet I'd think that jeans worn in public reflect poorly upon a well-reared lady.'

Henri to Marc: 'Isn't that a contradiction of terms?'

'Enough. We've work to do.' Serault placed a sheaf of papers on the table, unfolding the top one, a diagram of the casino. 'It's old but the details haven't changed much,' he explained, pointing with his finger. 'The entrance hall stretches along the north to the gaming rooms here, and the finance and security offices here. The hall also runs the length of the west wall that faces the Hôtel, and ends overlooking the terrace. It's flanked by bathrooms and La Salle Garnier, and the cloakroom which has a lift connecting to the Hôtel passage. The prince's private stairs come from the terrace at Avenue de Monte-Carlo, up to this landing and then to his theatre box. Dieter, could you move a little?'

Kalenberg shifting, the others crowding, Jennica standing behind Serault, who pushed his plate aside to make more room. 'Now, the terrace extends across the south side from the staircase to the entrance of the Black Jack Club on the eastern flank. In the club is another lift, and it's the only way besides the stairs to go directly up to the gaming rooms. By the way, the diagram shows a second, lower terrace, but a new hotel is being built there now. It used to be the old *Tir aux Pigeons* until the princess put a stop to the pigeon shooting.'

'Gave the sport a *coup de Grace*, eh?'

'Please, Wesley, a more mature attitude. All of you, note particularly the entrances to La Salle Garnier. One exit on the north hall and four on the west – two for the theatre itself, the next for the stage, and then the prince's stairs. You must become familiar with it, with all the casino. Visit it as often as you can.' Serault glanced around the table. 'During the gala, the casino will be closed to those without tickets. I understand the terrace will be glazed in frosty pink, a giant seashell erected for the stage, bandstand, and launch of the requisite fireworks display. With a big trident rising in the back, pronging streamers of sequined fishnet. If you don't know the meaning of kitsch you will when you see.'

Kalenberg asked: 'How many guards and detectives will we see?'

'Plenty, but the number's immaterial. If my idea works, it won't make any difference – if it doesn't, it'll make even less. The plan is based on SBM having taken the additional precaution this year to wire its entire security force for radio. Extras as well as regulars, transreceivers in the cruisers and walkie-talkies for the patrols and plainclothesmen.'

Ledoux, overtly sceptical. 'An entertaining theory.'

'Reliable fact. It all is. I know Monaco and I know the casino, and what I didn't know I judiciously asked. I've spent the past three days in research, browsing libraries, collecting maps, reading books and magazines. Society articles described why the gala will be safe. *Paris Match* reported the croupiers' strike over the installation of closed-circuit TV. And it so happens that the radio and TV is monitored and coordinated by a couple of dispatchers in the security office.'

Talmas rubbed his chin. 'After our lunch, didn't I remark . . . ?'

'Yes – that people can become dependent on electronics.'

Ledoux, stubbornly: 'René, the corridor leading to that office is notorious. It's long and purposely made the width of one man to stop any mass attacks. We'd never get down it and past the door.'

'Not all of us at once, true. But one of us could, I think, dressed as a guard. The dispatchers won't question an additional uniform out of so many unknown faces there for just the evening.'

'OK,' Talmas said. 'Assume we control the dispatchers so we control the whole force. But how do we control the regular police?'

'Again remember after our lunch, Wesley, when we saw that *Corps Urbain* painter? Their little vans are parked nightly in the police garages, either at the substation on

Avenue Princess Alice or the headquarters in La Condamine. Now, we find out which numbered Vespas go to where, then sabotage one for each basement garage. At the right moment – explosion, fire, smoke. Firemen invading the stations. The police evacuating, diverted by being the diversions themselves.'

Henri grinning: 'Worse than if hit by a sullen tomato.'

'Only a miser like you could invent such a two-for-one ploy.' Ledoux filled Serault's glass. 'Have some wine, I'm impressed.'

'It's beastly,' Jennica said. 'It sounds worse than war. What if the prince or princess were hurt, René?'

'I'm not an anarchist, chérie. Nothing will start until after they've left for the palace, which traditionally is three-quarters through the gala, around one a.m. This will protect them. And us from their personal bodyguards, who're homicidal when disturbed. During the lull that always follows, security will be less attentive, the guests lazy from food and drink. Distracted, perhaps, by the confusion outside the casino. They'll readily submit at the sight of our guns.'

'One look at my Stens will intimate them.'

'Regrettably, Marc, the Stens are too bulky to smuggle inside. But as a convincer, we'll take hostages and threaten to shoot them.'

Jennica, agitated: 'Why, why they could be killed.'

'Not they, chérie, you. You and the guard will be our hostages, to clear you of complicity and give an excuse for accompanying us.'

'Pisstaking,' she whispered. 'And how do we escape?'

'By helicopter, since the roads and sea are too slow and will be blocked. Bernard will pilot, flying from his yard when we signal.'

'Insanity,' Ledoux snapped. 'I can always give Fifine an excuse why a copter's stowed in my yard – she'll be merely impossible. But an international alert will be broadcast the instant we lift off the terrace. The Gendarmes, the Marine Nationale, the Aviation based at Toulon –'

'Hyères. Where I found a seven-seat Alouette III for rent.'

60

'The south pole! Jets will be here before we're anywhere else.'

'Not before we can reach the hills where radar can't track us. Marc, Henri, you know the Alpine valleys best. Where's a short hop from Monaco that's desolate, yet that we can drive out from?'

The brothers consulted, Marc finally saying: 'There's an abandoned quarry up past Sospel near the Nieya River. The truck lane into it might still be passable. It's only a big hole.'

'Well worth checking,' Serault said. 'So assume we land there. We then bury our good fortune for later disinterment and drive away.'

'Oyez! We'd still be digging when the cops arrived.'

Kalenberg: 'I've heard that the disposing is the most dangerous time of all.'

'I admit it isn't fully planned.' Serault extending placative hands. 'And that's why we're meeting, to work out the nuances. But we've got to begin with what we have, or we'll never be ready in time. And Dieter, you've been hearing myths, rumours spread to discourage thieves. Actually, collectors pay high prices, owners rebuy favourites, police reward returned goods, and insurance firms pay a percentage to trim claims. All of them eager and discreet. The dross left over can be extracted and sold en masse. Switzerland is reputedly the best market, according to those who buy not sell.'

Ledoux teetering in his chair, back to grasp the umbrella pole beside him for support. 'Not quite so fast, René, I'm far from convinced. Your theory is that we control the casino and distract the police and firemen. But help could be summoned lots of other ways.'

'Indeed, and probably would be.' Serault brought out an area map. 'For example, TV-Monte-Carlo transmits from Mont-Agel, 11 kilometres north of Monaco. Their radio tower is closer, on Mont-Gros.'

Marc shook his head. 'The section is all military and closed.'

'Not entirely,' Serault said. 'Hikers are allowed on the

trail going to the top of Mont-Agel. I'm counting on our army being too concerned with its own radar and missiles to notice a stray backpacker dropping plastique among the Principality's property.'

'What about telephone and telegraph?' Kalenberg asked.

'Well, I argued with an operator over poor connections,' Serault explained, 'and learned there's only one trunk line serving Monaco. The cable surfaces for repairs at a P & T branch on Rue de la Colle. Their central pick-up is at four; if, on the night of the gala, a bomb were mailed just before closing at six, it would stay there.'

'Until it went off,' Henri said. 'How about the power lines?'

'We don't cut them. All of Monaco's water and electricity is supplied by France, and a sudden cut or blackout would bring instant response. We want to cause paralysis and indecision, not intervention.'

'Why,' Talmas asked, 'wouldn't you French interfere anyway?'

'Politics,' Serault replied. 'A friendly sub rosa rivalry exists between us, as sometimes can happen between relatives.'

'Not always so friendly or sub,' Ledoux said. 'Recall in '62, René, when De Gaulle blockaded their customs? You've a valid point; our gendarmes and Sûreté Nationale would be reluctant to come uninvited.'

'Also, the casino has its own generator.' Serault shuffled the diagram on top again. 'Directly to the left of the entrance, here, is an unmarked door leading to the basement power and work rooms.'

Kalenberg gleamed, like a banker's eye. 'And to the vault?'

'Forget the vault. America has Fort Knox, Monte Carlo has The Big V. However, the gala attracts all the big players, and their money plus most of the vault's will be in the tables' cashboxes. Also, in the basement is the private back entrance to Von Cleef & Arpels.'

'We'll rob it along with the gala?' Marc laughed.

'No, René. There's bound to be alarms going off.'

'Dieter, I once said nothing bad is publicized in Monaco. Hence, no horns or bells are allowed to jangle wealthy nerves. Silent alarms, yes, but where? In the empty police stations and the security office.'

'Birdlime,' Talmas said.

'I beg your pardon.'

'Sorry, René, a blurt. I was thinking of the view from my window: of Van Cleef's. Yeah, and the other stuff I've seen.' He took off his glasses and massaged his eyes. 'The greed of crime, hey?'

'Wesley, you tempt me to say – No, it'd cause you distress.'

'No more than already, René.'

'Ah well. I had another plan to rob Cartier, the Hôtel deposit boxes and the Horsten display.' Serault pausing – a general recoil, including Ledoux thumping down in his chair – then he hunkered forward sighing. 'It required my car to look like an ambulance and Bernard to drive it. He alone having the proper licence, no use trifling with roadblocks. But he can't drive and fly at the same time.'

Talmas stopped rubbing his eyes. 'My interest in planes isn't entirely academic, René. I've a valid private pilot rating.'

'You can fly?'

Talmas nodding, squinting craftily. 'I've never tackled a helo before, though some buddies flew me in a Bell 47 and swore that once it was up, it handled just like a Cessna 150.'

Serault turned to Ledoux. 'Bernard, could you teach him?'

'I'm unsure of my own rusty abilities. How can I answer?'

'This surely deserves a try,' Serault urged. 'Look: when the Family is leaving the gala, the Place du Casino will be flooded with sightseers. The Hôtel lobby will be deserted except for the concierge and a clerk, a porter maybe, and the Horsten guard.'

'Assuming this, René,' Ledoux asked, 'what do we do with them?'

'Involuntary exile to a back room. After we pick the boxes and display, we'll break into Cartier through the wall of the Empire Room. From there, we'll go on to the gala, while you speed away, flasher and siren, with the bijouterie we've collected.'

'Or you four, more dead than alive.'

'Stop quibbling, Bernard. Don't you understand we've got the choice? From preparation to finish, if one part sours or the next smells suspicious, we move to something else or quit completely. If the lobby is full, we go straight to Cartier's. If Wesley can't learn in time, we forget this section and concentrate on the gala.'

'A few lessons, then.' Ledoux sighing, musing aloud: 'And the Citroën can be camouflaged . . . a fortunate similarity of contour . . . Should rent a garage near the Hôtel, safer and quicker for driving . . .'

'A garage, Bernard, a fine suggestion. And get together with Dieter. We need something to detonate primers by remote control.'

'Yes,' Kalenberg answered instead. 'Electronically possible.'

'Also, Jennica must be able to signal us from the gala.'

'There's tone-calls small enough to fit in her purse, René. However, I think I'll have to drive to Paris for some of the supplies.'

'I'd like to come along, Dieter,' Jennica said. 'To choose my costume jewellery; Kenny Lane fakes, I suppose. Also material and theatrical make-up . . .' She tilted her head, regarding the men. 'I'll have to measure and study all of you beforehand, of course.'

'Mascara! Rouge! To be painted like a rocking horse.'

'There's nothing swish or crude about this, Dieter,' she retorted. 'The disguising is to fool the casino guards and physiogonomists. Effects and illusion is the crux, not silly masquerade costuming.'

'The description of us will be false,' Serault said. 'Plus the gala will be too chaotic to untangle later who was where when. We will be lambs twice innocent and shorn with the rest. Eh, and speaking of later: to avoid being traced afterwards, we probably should buy everything in Paris. Different stores, ordinary items. Thin leather gloves, adhesive tape, black jeweller's satchels, pillow cases, an intern's smock for Bernard, a stretcher and sheet – '

'René,' Marc interrupted. 'Draping a sheet over the stretcher will not hide a mountain of jewels. It must appear natural.'

'A body, you advise? One we somehow stuff like a partridge?'

'How about . . .' Ledoux said slowly '. . . a *poupée gonflable*?'

Talmas stared at him. 'One of those blow-up girl dolls?'

'Right,' Serault responded. 'A virtual inner tube. I recommend the deluxe blonde with matching hair down there where you – with hair.'

'The standard is cheaper.'

'But Bernard, if a cop peeked under the cover, he'd think she was shaved indecently. He might wish to investigate.'

'*Die Kletschbase Zeitung* has advertisements for models with batterized variable-pitch oscillating and contracting action.'

'Marvellous, the German dedication to impotency cures.'

'And guaranteed a year against burn-out and puncture.'

'Poisonous,' Jennica flared. 'I could kick both of you.'

'Knee-jerk of a feminist, but anything to keep the peace. Dieter, one plastic lady at your discretion. Or indiscretion. And add tuxedoes to the list, to be bought not rented for obvious reasons.'

Ledoux was drumming his fingers pensively. 'Tuxedoes, helicopters, and of course the tickets. It's going to be expensive, René.'

'We must invest what we can, Bernard.'

'You expect me to mortgage my yard for this?'

'If necessary,' Serault said, 'and with the proper sangfroid.'

'Well, I'm game,' Talmas said, 'as long as it isn't my sang-chaud that spills. Worth gambling on what I've heard so far.'

'We've barely begun, Wesley.' Serault lifting the champagne by its dripping neck. 'A sip or two and we'll spend the afternoon ironing out the minutiae.' Unwinding the wire, the pop of the cork. Everybody watching the brown mushroom sail over the edge of the terrace and arc towards the excavation below. Serault pouring froth in the special glasses Jennica had dealt. Standing with glass extended :

'Be happy. Don't worry about a miscarriage later. We're contemplating the largest nongovernmental theft in history, and there aren't many who are capable of this much. Of every politician, publicity hack and encyclopedia salesman, we are automatically the envy. Celebrate. Accept our condition. We're crooks.'

Chapter Nine

Sultry mid-morning, La Condamine resinous with exhaust, commerce, mental aspirations. Swifts wheeling above shrubbery, waiters flicking at desultory flies and tourists. The Vattiers unhooking a two-wheel tar wagon from the back of a van, a Citroën *camionette* which had come from Ledoux's yard. The tar wagon much abused, coated with years, reeking and bubbling from a vesuvian burner underneath. Buckets, brooms and brushes clustered with tools and tar-paper in a front compartment: which bore the sign: GREFFE CONSTRUCTEURES ET CIE.

Henri pulled the trailer hitch, Marc pushing from behind, awkwardly avoiding being gelded by a rear spigot. The wagon wobbled by the side of the Sûreté Publique headquarters, a five-storey stucco cube defiantly mundane. Past its basement garage ramp, flanked by pump and sentry. Turning left on Rue Suffren Reymond, the main entrance a few metres ahead, the block ending at Boulevard Albert 1er and a harbour of swaying masts.

'To the No Parking Zone,' Marc panted. 'Behind that British car . . .' Both brothers were winded, wishing they could have driven around if only for a moment to unhitch. But even if there were no trouble today, should a bored cop glance at the truck now, its licence might be traced later . . . 'Here, Henri, set it down. Henri? Set it down.'

'I have.'

'Balourd!' The wagon with inexorable momentum dragged the vainly braking Vattiers, ploughing the hitch over yielding pavement. Into the conservative trunk of a stolid black Wolseley sedan. A distinguished crunch. Hastily they scouted the survivors and witnesses – 'Quick now, before we're seen – ' rolled off the wagon and examined the damage – 'Luckily the colour is dark.' Henri took a brush handle to the tail pipe, prying it down and open. Marc smoothed the dent with lumps of tar and deft fudgings with a broom, then swiftly to the wagon spigot to draw a bucket of asphalt.

'Just pray the owner is blind,' Marc said, while Henri snatched up a tarpaper roll to go with his brush. Marc brought the bucket around and hefted a long metal toolkit by its shoulder strap. 'How Papa would have loved being here, eh, Henri? As he always used to say, hit 'em where they hurt.'

Fording the street and sidewalk. Through the portal of swing-doors, paper slipping, toolkit barking paint from the jamb. Up the steps to the lobby, four Agents de Sûreté Publique craning to view so inelegant an entry. The Vattiers ignoring them. Briskly crossing the clean waxed floor, impatient labourers on errands too important to be disturbed. Especially by the Officer on Duty, who sat thin, hunched, a mantis at his PBX switchboard, talking to a large woman whose talcumed bosom shadowed a man of pullover and weedy pipe:

'. . . You allege, Madame, a girl propositioned your husband while your back was turned. With what result? One moment – You!'

Marc locking in midstop. 'Us, sir?'

'Who else is here? And why?'

'To repair the roof. You've been notified, of course.'

'I haven't. And I don't see any note of it here.'

The PBX buzzed. A flurry of toggles and cables, the officer answering: 'Oui, Commandant. Yvonne? Non . . . Oui . . .' And he unplugged to ask: 'Have any of you seen the Commandant's old bitch?'

'Nigel,' the woman sucked in. 'Did you hear?'

The quartet of agents shaking their heads, a ferret-like one saying, 'She's probably loose in the district again, begging.'

The officer nodding. 'And he's afraid she'll contract a disease.'

'How uncouth, Nigel.' And Nigel's pipe wagging up and down, a silent tongue.

'Maurice,' the officer said to the agent, 'it's your turn to find his spaniel. Now!' And the agent touched stiff fingers to his cap, moving towards the entrance with a sigh of tiredness and rue. The officer once more regarding the Vattiers. 'You, where's your authorization? Who told you to come here anyway? Our roof is fine.'

'The prince,' Marc said.

Official eyebrows arched. 'The prince?'

'Himself. Saw from the Rock and declared it an insult and a menace. But we'll leave; we were to've finished by lunchtime anyway.'

'As short a job as that.'

'A patching. But since petty regulations are more important . . .'

'I could phone for confirmation.'

'Would you, sir. Insinuate we're dishonest while he dines.'

The officer mulled, then nosed forward, a cynic beadle. 'Right. Some advice, however. Straight to the roof and straight back down, or I'll arrange a more permanent detour than you had in mind.'

'As an arrow. No frolicking in the halls, sir, on my word.'

Smartly accelerating with a tug of forelocks. Loading the lift which was paltry and self-serving, an uncomfortable squeeze for the brothers and their gear. To the top floor, a long corridor of diffused lighting and office doors. Trundling along, they cast a quick glance at the door plaques or into the open rooms. Clerks and typists and junior-grade uniforms, the hum of well-lubricated wheels grinding fine. Arson. Vice. Communications. The office of the Commandant Principal, its door abruptly opening, a pretty girl tripping out and into Henri, who shied, tarpaper drooping, one end of the roll nudging the lip of the bucket. Which ever so slightly tipped. To pour a generous blob of tar unnoticed on the floor.

'Excuse us,' Marc said. 'We're trying to get to the roof.'

'It's through that door over there.'

'Thanks. And where'll you be going later, say about six or seven?'

'Home to my husband who's a sergeant.'

'You don't say, and it's been nice to chat.'

Through the door and up the last few steps to the shedlike exit on the roof. Across a sunburnt sea of asbestos, avoiding islands of pipes and ducts, the radio mast midway, the jetsam of birds. To the large housing for the lift and air-conditioning systems. The strum of cables, the drone of ventilators, the Vattiers shedding their flotsam next to a metre-square air-intake grille.

'It's laid out up here pretty much as we'd hoped,' Henri said.

'Logical. A building's a building, a roof's a roof.' Marc removing screwdriver, prybar, and a shoebox from his tool-kit. The box was cardboard reinforced with a plywood base to which Alnico magnets were attached. 'You take the grille off, I'll do the rest.'

Leaving Henri, Marc went to the radio aerial. Bringing out another box, which was smaller and of metal, with U-bolts instead of magnets and with two insulated electrical jacks, one at each end. He clamped the box to the mast and was unscrewing the box's faceplate when he paused to glare at his brother, who was pacing back and forth for no particular reason.

'Stop it, Henri. You're driving me rogue.'

'I don't like it, putting yours on the mast where it's so obvious.'

'No place to hide it, is there? But it sort of looks as though it belongs this way, like it's a signal booster or something.'

Marc removing the plate. Rubbing his hands while peering inside, at: most of the circuitry from a common walkie-talkie; 12 volts' worth of batteries; the 9-volt solenoid from a household doorbell, its bell-clapper rod soldered to the trigger of a standard mouse trap: and a 12-gauge shotgun

70

shell, its pellets replaced by a wad of plastique. Gingerly Marc pulled the trap's spring back, cocking it. He eyed it charily as he took from the toolkit a coil of lampcord, a stub of a nail, and a telescoping antenna, the kind used on transistor radios. He extended the antenna and plugged it into the top jack. Then eased the nail into the primer pocket at the base of the shotgun shell.

Henri was standing well away, over near the northern parapet. 'Hey, I can see Wesley Talmas from here. He's up at the corner of Rue Grimaldi, wearing a sports shirt the colour of his sunburn.'

'What's he doing?' Marc asked, rescrewing the face plate.

'Nothing. He may stay that way.'

'He's too nervous.' Marc plugged one end of the cord into the bottom jack and began unreeling a line across the roof. 'But Talmas has heart.'

'What he's missing is a little lower and to the right.'

'No, he'll act when necessary, when he's too busy to worry.' Squatting by the duct now, grille off and shoebox stuck to the metal lip. 'Go and brush some tar over the cord, Henri, but for God's sake don't bump the mast.' Marc took off the lid of the box. Inside was another solenoid and mouse trap, and one of their cache's old signal flares. The flare had a friction cap to ignite it, and the cap's pull-tab was crimped to the trap spring. Marc set the trap, replaced the box lid and wound masking tape around it, and refitted the grille.

'There.' Marc standing, hands on hips. 'Now if only they'll work as planned. I don't trust any of it, Henri.'

'Dieter swears his design is foolproof.'

A gathering of equipment and to the exit, evading the freshly painted tar. Down the stairs and into the corridor, rolling smugly until coming to the Commandant's door. Where they hesitated, curious about the chunk of tar. Wedged into it now was the sole of a shoe, a polished black oxford, unlaced and tongue lolling, so that it resembled the pedestal of a Winged Mercury, Mercury having flown.

'I think, Henri, we'd best move on.'

'With haste, Marc, with haste.'

Into the lift and downwards with thoughts of how many candles should be lit if a church could be reached for sanctuary. The lobby appeared normal, quieter than before. The Vattiers steaming lively for the entrance, a cursory nod while passing the officer on duty. The officer glancing their way briefly before speaking into the phone again:

'No, sir . . . No, I swear, I have no idea what Yvonne could have eaten to have caused such a thing . . .'

Chapter Ten

Wesley T.

Crossing Rue Sufferin Reymond with a plastic shopping bag, in search of a Vespa triwheeler. Any one of half a dozen vans scattered about on duty would do, their numbers etched on a paper folded in his pocket and engraved on his brain along with presentiments of disaster. Of something fearful happening to him or Jennica, who had a list of the vans from the substation garage, or to one of the other men. If not now then later, after their preparations were complete, due to an unforeseen disaster or a problem that refused to be solved – such as what they'd do once at the quarry, a detail so far unanswered and seemingly as elusive as the Vespas.

Trekking fatigued and mentally perturbed up Rue Grimaldi. Long windows with iron bars set in paint-blistered walls, postcard racks shivering in the wake of buses and trucks. Instamatics, lotions, laxatives, and Ellery Queen mysteries under the melancholy twilight of awnings. Talmas slowing . . . stopping. Parked ahead, beside a boutique, was a Vespa number 313 and on his list.

He approached warily; no sign of the driver or other uniformed menaces. Peered into the boutique, where a pubescent salesgirl was telling a matron no the dress did not come in size 44 but it will stretch madam. Another jaundiced survey of the sidewalks and stores, but still only tourists in view. Jesus, there just wasn't any way around this other than attack it.

Talmas knelt beside the van. Feeling nostalgia as well as

aversion, 313 being the licence plate of Donald Duck's rumble-seat roadster. From his bag he removed a metal box – like the one Marc had placed on the radio mast, but with both plastique and a flare inside, and instead of clamps, magnets which clung to the Vespa's belly-pan when he slipped it underneath. Very tenderly so, the dual mouse traps having been pre-set. Of similar colour and grime, the box blended with the chassis, and barring quirks of fate like motor overhauls and thumping big potholes, it should remain undetected and untriggered until signalled during the gala, the night after tomorrow. A theory not improving Talmas's serenity.

Because a telescoping antenna would be too noticeable, a thin wire had been rigged to the box as an aerial. Talmas pulled the wire taut and began attaching it along the lower rim of the van with daubs of putty-like adhesive, working quickly yet feeling time stretch to a frustrating eternity. A bead of perspiration trickled down his forehead, into his eye. Stinging. It wasn't that he lacked the courage or resolve, but if only he had some of René's sense of destiny. Or Dieter's dedication or Jennica's insouciance or those bullock brothers' mountain machismo or even Bernard's wife. His incentive was mere desire. For a fleet of jets and bourbon in the office water cooler and pubescent secretaries after hours telling him yes and it will stretch sir. Of capital importance that, executive privilege . . .

Abruptly he was aware of company. A shadow crossing the sidewalk in front of him, and the scrape of glossy boots. Talmas looked up, at dark blue trousers with a crease capable of cutting butter, a slightly lighter blue shirt, a face reminding him of a ferret, and a white cap with a chrome badge like an evil eye. And Talmas experienced that instant spasm of martyrdom, when blood jells and flesh dissolves and absolute despair grips the coil of one's mortality.

The policeman leaned forward to ask in French: 'Have you seen a passing spaniel?'

Talmas, not understanding: 'I'm tying my shoe.'

In English: 'M'sieu, you're wearing loafers.'

'Yes, so I am. Well, reconsidering, I suffer from the sensation of having an untied shoe.'

'But why're you holding that wire?'

'Must be what caused the effect of the shoelace.'

'Indeed. Replace it on the van. This instant.'

Talmas fixed the wire and stood up, blinking and stunned.

The policeman held out his hand. 'The bag, M'sieu.' Taking, looking down inside. At nothing. Returning it, disappointed. 'Still, scavenging of official property while under the influence. I'd run you in if it weren't for the fact nobody in Monaco is ever intoxicated. And my orders to find the spaniel. Have you seen her?'

'No sir.'

'That I don't doubt. I'd better not see you again, either.'

Talmas hurried away. To catch a bus conveniently passing, and sit in a stupor of aftershock, finally getting off nowhere near where he was to meet Jennica, and consequently being an hour late for their rendezvous on Avenue de la Costa. Where he waited a short while until she arrived in her mini. She leaned across to open the door for him, and he slid in beside her. They wheeled from the kerb and she asked:

'What took you so long? I was going to go around this Grand Prix circuit three more times and then you could bloody well walk.'

'Something came up.'

'I didn't have a speck of trouble,' she said as if not hearing him. 'I found my van and was done in fifteen minutes. Stopped for a snack, an Assiette Anglaise according to the menu. A typical French insult; it was a plate of cold meats. What came up?'

'A cop while I was putting on the wire.'

'Oh no.' Jennica stared at him deflated against the seat.

'Well, I think it turned out all right.' Talmas lapsed silent, grateful he was alive to still feel disturbed about the incident, and smell the warm engine and sense the gathering speed. Away through the plundered skyline and towards Roquebrune. He watched how Jennica drove with a waspish impetus, bare-limbed and sensually basic in shorts and bolero.

75

'René must be told,' he added lamely. 'The worst part is personal. I froze. Completely went to pieces.'

'I'm sure you acted perfectly, if only subconsciously.' Patting him on the leg, sympathetically and not high up, but sufficiently to make him react with a rising and embarrassing urgency. He turned away to stare out of the open side window at oncoming traffic.

One of the sixty-ton dump trucks from Serault's rock garden lumbered past. Squeezing pneumatic brakes, a grey sulphurous belch from its exhaust pipe lancing against Talmas's face and filling the interior. God-damned trucks ought to be . . .

Ought to be . . .

An idea stabbed at Talmas, persisting through fits of choking, and when at last the haze had cleared, he realized he'd coughed up an answer to the problem of the quarry. Talmas straightened with a curious tension to his pose. Feeling more vindicated than elated, his personal merit restored and his value as a partner redeemed, and yet unsure if it weren't just a momentary tonic.

. . . Roquebrune. They knocked on the front door, which was answered by Ledoux. 'Good. René and Dieter are on the terrace and Marc just phoned. They're returning the tar wagon before it's missed. How do I look?'

He shut the door and they walked through the house, Jennica regarding him with a professional air. His moustache had been shaved off, a false one being worn until the real grew back after the gala. 'Bernard, you look quite natural. You've mastered it.'

'I've been practising. Though last night it fell off in bed and my wife killed it with her shoe, mistaking it for a centipede.'

'Lord. Didn't she see your bare lip?'

'Luckily, Jennica, Fifine had her mouth open wider than her eyes. She's been giving me some odd glares though, and I think she suspects something is up if only in a general way . . .'

Through the living room, onto the terrace, where Renè

76

lounged atop a mound of tie-died Moroccan cushions like a Byzantine pimp. He was crosshatched with scratches, as many scratches as there was bare skin, with a swollen blotch beside his nose and closing his left eye. His right eye, pink and beery, was directed at a greatly diminished bottle of wine, and at Kalenberg sitting with a 5 inch fibreglass attaché case open on his generous lap. Kalenberg was explaining the case when interrupted by Jennica:

'René! What on earth!'

'Nothing.'

'Your eye!'

'Nothing, I tell you. Listen to Dieter.'

'Guten-tag, Jennica, Wesley. As I was saying, Bernard and – '

'But your bruises, your cuts!'

'Never mind, woman, business comes first. Continue, Dieter.'

' – I chose Johnson model 125 walkie-talkies because they're common and have a long range. And a built-in tone-coded squelch, which allows a unit to run silently until keyed by another unit of the same frequency and tone-call. Essentially, each of our charges has a receiver and squelch section that matches a transmitter and tone-call in this case. To operate, extend this antenna and switch on this 12-volt lantern battery. From it lots of power, including for the receiver that'll buzz whenever Jennica signals. On this panel, each button is for a separate tone-call and corresponding squelch, and I've retuned each pair's frequency to prevent random interference tripping them, and so that pushing one button won't set them all off together. You can trigger the charges in any sequence you desire. When keyed, the squelch opens a power circuit to the doorbell solenoid. The rest is self-evident.'

'We wanted to use electric detonating caps to save time and space,' Ledoux said. 'But at this late date, they're impossible to steal much less buy without a permit.'

'Well, you and Dieter cooked up a damn nifty alternative.'

'We did what we could with what we could get,' Kalenberg said proudly. 'And how was your morning?'

'No, René first,' Jennica cut in sharply. 'René, you left at dawn to hike to Mont Agel. Look at you now. What happened?'

'Exactly what was supposed to happen. I placed a charge at the television cable relay – don't want the actual tower to come crashing down, of course, too much commotion that way. Next I went down and across to the radio tower, keeping off the secondary path since it was Private No Trespassing, yet parallel to it so I could see any Authorized Personnel Only before they saw me.'

'Renè, stop evading the issue.'

'I tell my stories my own way. Where was I? Well, I was almost back to the main trail again when I chanced upon a blackberry thicket heavy with ripe fruit. Naturally I picked some, but I overreached, lost my balance and pitched down among the roots. Into a nest of squealing piglets. Then I heard their mother coming to protect her brood, and they weren't piglets, they were wild boars.'

Jennica looked faintly appalled. 'Did she run after you?'

Serault nodded, burrowing deeper into the cushions. 'No cover, no protection, just that bramble, a few pines with their first branches way over my head, thistle and gorse. I ran for the only possible shelter, an outhouse erected on the main trail to discourage hikers from defoliating the shrubbery. There was a narrow vent high on the back wall, and I was trying to squeeze free when she hit the door, crushing it flat, and charged the one-hole seat I was using to stand on. Gored it to splinters. The wall fell out with me stuck half through the vent, the roof fell on the boar, and the boar fell in the pit.'

'Oh poor love, I'll rub some oint-'

'Don't touch me. Nothing's broken or twisted, I merely sprained a few unused muscles.' Serault groaned while reaching for the wine. 'Stop playing nurse and tell us if you had any trouble this morning.'

'*I* didn't.' Jennica rolling her eyes Talmas-ward, Talmas fighting, clearing his throat and patting the change in his pocket and finally saying, 'While I was attaching the wire, a cop came along.'

Serault grimaced. Ledoux smiled. Kalenberg winced and carefully closed the lid of the attaché case. 'There it goes.'

'Wait. The cop didn't arrest me or even ask who I was.'

'No, there it goes and I'm half a step behind it.'

'Let me explain. He suspected I was drunk and stripping the van as a prank. That and something about a dog I didn't quite get. He ordered me to put the wire on – back on, you see? He never tumbled.'

Serault closed his one eye. '*Were* you drunk?'

'Aw Jesus no.' Talmas gesturing uncomfortably. 'I think it's OK, I really do. If I didn't, I'd be on a plane by now if I had to hijack the bastard. But my bomb is in place and I bet the ass has forgotten all about me. Though it's your decision, René.'

Serault did not speak for some time. Wrapped in, or more precisely unwrapped by, Talmas's admission, its inherent pathos as well as danger . . . My decision. Possibly a pivotal one, and I sense my own self-confidence ebbing, leaving behind a gradual apprehension, so that small patches like this assume undue proportion. All the more rationale to plunge on. To falter now would make my life fully instead of mostly insupportable . . .

At last: 'I agree, Wesley. If you'd been important enough *not* to forget, you'd have been arrested. Moreover, you say the cop hasn't your name, and as your sport shirt could blind a seeing-eye dog, I'm sure it'll be all he'll remember if pressed later.'

'I won't wear the shirt again. I'm sorry, René, honest I am.'

'I suggest we forget it along with the cop. There're certain unpreventables, as most of us have learned one way or another. Did you pace off the fresco and service pantry in the Empire Room?'

'During dinner last night,' Talmas answered. 'The left-hand panel is hidden by the pantry, as you know, but the right one looks the same and is about three metres wide. The pantry partition is nearly six long, and its doorway is just over one metre wide. Oh – and against the fresco in the pantry was a counter and some glass racks.'

'Did you find anything that'll fit the doorway?'

'Well, the closet door in my room will, and it comes off its hinges easily. But if we snatch one from upstairs someplace, it'll draw attention to the job having been pulled by a Hôtel guest. However, the door to the men's room also fits, is closer, and well, is sort of public domain there off the lobby.'

'The men's room it is. Bernard, will you go with Wesley this afternoon and take measurements, especially for the hinges?'

'Just stroll in and whip out my tape measure?'

'Whip out whatever you like, but we must have exact specifications for the Vattiers to build an adjustable doorframe that'll work. And are you positive my Citroën will be finished for the morning?'

'I am positive it has been for years. Otherwise, I can only repeat what I told you when I arrived – the false licence plates are on, and assuming the garage we rented doesn't have rain, your car is drying to a ghastly violet.' Ledoux turned to Jennica and Talmas, explaining: 'You see, because of all the quick alterations, I'm spraying on water-soluble colours that will wash clean between changes.'

'Now,' Serault said, 'we should leave by nine tomorrow if we're to reach Hyères airport by eleven-thirty. I'd hate to be late for our own dress rehearsal.'

Jennica said, 'Watch that none of us drink from the wine bottle that has an X on the label. I've dissolved all of René's barbiturates in it. Oh, and Dieter? I'll need a final costume fitting for you.'

'Don't call me Dieter. Call me now Erich von Beverstadt.'

Serault sighed. 'Tomorrow is too soon to call anybody such an insufferable alias. But taking the whole thing on balance, things look well. The odds against our adventure may have slightly increased, but without a direct link to Wesley T. I doubt the risk of capture has.' Stroking his neck, gazing about dolefully. 'We're left with only one major dilemma. Once at the quarry, what then?'

'I hate to dampen the mood with my ideas,' Talmas said.

'If they're stronger than a prayer, we'll consider them.'

'René, your faith sustains me, but listen. We've agreed we take the loot with us, because sure as hell the cops will fine-tooth the quarry with metal detectors. We can't use cars because of the weight – imagine arguing at a road-block with our axles dragging – we can't stay in the area because that's the first place they'll be hunting, and we can't cross into Italy because that's the first place they'll be hunting too. So by a process of elimination, what we must do is drive a huge truck right down to here.'

Ledoux, dawning: 'We double in, they search out there.'

'A feint . . .' Serault poked an idle finger into the bottle. 'It'd take two trucks since there're six of us. Dressed as labourers, including Jennica, and using some of those old identity cards the Vattiers cribbed . . . Appealing, Wesley, but to where exactly down here?'

'*Here*. We're planning to have Bernard stash the doll in your basement, so why not dig a big hole for the whole kaboodle? The dirt can go over the side into the excavation; it'll never be noticed.'

'But where do the trucks come from?' Kalenberg asked. 'And how do we return them in time? They're not dirt. They'd be noticed.'

Talmas thumbed towards the terrace edge. 'Those guys down there quit when, at six? Henri and Marc could liberate a couple of dump-trucks afterwards, park them at the quarry and be at the gala by eleven. It'd take five minutes to return them Saturday morning.'

'You realize the peculiarly satisfying justice to using SBM trucks,' Serault gloated. 'Better yet, one will be a cement-mixer. We can hide everything in it, and, moreover, be able to pour everything directly into my *cave* without attracting attention. Then cover with a tarp and a layer of concrete. And it also solves how we can be innocently back here on the scene, a must by dawn at the latest.'

81

'To think,' Jennica said, 'the answer was under our noses.'

'Under our bottoms,' Ledoux said. 'It sounds good to me.'

Kalenberg said, 'Somehow not to me. It's too logical.'

Talmas, miffed: 'Is that a reason or twinges of lumbago?'

'I mistrust it, that's all, a feeling I've the right to express.'

'But we've got to decide and quickly,' Serault said. 'I think we should try Wesley's idea.' He relapsed into a veiled sort of meditation, quiet and eye closed until the others began to grow impatient and worry he'd fallen asleep. Then, softly, he added: 'I hope you're wrong, Dieter. At any rate, we should have a fair idea by tomorrow night . . .'

Chapter Eleven

Fade in: which is motion picture jargon for the opening shot.

Fade in on a violet station wagon driving southwest from Roquebrune and Monaco on the Moyenne Corniche, winding among cliffs of a fierce titian contrast to the tepid sea below. Entering Nice, speeding along the port and Le Promenade des Anglais, leaving to curve inland on Autoroute de l'Estérel and avoid the glut of Antibes and Cannes. Link ing west of Fréjus with old N-7, a black two-lane river flowing through the plain of Argens, to Le Luc and coast-ward again on N-97. And to track the car as it threads sluggish high-season kilometres of crash helmets and trucks with tandem trailers and motorists arguing over collisions. Then the cutoff at LaFarlède, joining N-98 and into Hyères, where an officer in his intersection pulpit was conducting a white-gloved adagio. Exit Hyères, angling towards the beaches and the Giens Peninsula, for the Toulon airport at Hyères is not at Hyères but in an outlying marsh of marram grass known as La Palyvestre.

Zoom in on the Citroën, speckled with squashed insects. Serault at the wheel, glazed and sour from the hours of traffic, countenance hidden and itching behind an anarchist's bristly beard. Beside him was Jennica, now bigger breasted, black wigged and bound in a crocheted minidress fitting her on the principle of stretch tights. Behind, Talmas was wearing Ledoux's pencil moustache and a wig of matching colour. He attempted crossing his legs, but was too tightly hemmed by Ledoux and Kalenberg, and was forced to settle for wiping his brow with the sleeve of his shirt. Ledoux, tinted tan enough to be Levantine, alternated between adjusting Talmas's glasses on his nose, smoothing his monogrammed shirt over candy-striped slacks, and feigning disinterest in having lost the dapper clothing sweepstakes to Kalenberg: who kept flexing an alligator-skin riding crop, lounging resplendent in cord jodphurs, high-top boots, red check shirt, cream stock pinned with a pearl horseshoe, and a panama hat concealing the fact of his baldness.

The Citroën swayed as it rounded the entrance to the airport. Swayed again as it straightened along the driveway. An Air-Inter Caravelle landing nearby, flaps down and wheels locked. Serault cursed over the thunder of the jet: 'Shit, the 11.55 from Paris.'

'Impossible,' Ledoux said. 'You've driven like a Belgian.'

'Nevertheless, we're half an hour late. Dammit, this is the only airport close enough with a helicopter of suitable size; we miss our appointment here and we can forget all our plans except the gala itself.'

'I know you blame me,' Kalenberg said. 'But the leading man has to be allowed extra time to prepare his entrance.'

'You?' Ledoux glared sideways. 'You're the most expendable, Dieter. René arranged the rental, Talmas and I for the obvious reason, and Jennica to return the barge. You contribute only flamboyant ballast.'

'Jealousy and spite. Who else could portray my role with its required dignity, with its necessary weight?'

'True, true. In America we'd call your part the heavy.'

'Wesley, no insolence from you either. Particularly as this entire roadshow risks bombing out during your debut as test pilot.'

'Don't worry about me flying that bird. I'm positive I can.'

Kalenberg brandished his crop: 'If yesterday's fiasco with the police is an example of your judgement, I remain unconvinced.'

The drive looped in an oval before the passenger building – low, bland, with a central tower looming at the far end. Serault parked and everybody got out including Jennica, to whom he said: 'No reason to come in with us, chérie. You should start back.'

'Hardly. I want to observe the reactions to my disguises.'

She handed Serault a bulky flight-bag and led the procession into the marble lobby, where she waited for Serault to catch up and tell her: 'You are jeopardizing yourself needlessly, Jennica.'

'You said this was to be our dress rehearsal, René, and it should be mine as well. I insist, and it's rather late to argue.'

Serault sighed the male sigh of capitulation, and directed them through a gauntlet of ticket counters, advertisements, candy machines, and a clot of people waiting listlessly to depart on the Air Alpes flight for Ajaccio. Almost to the rear boarding gates there was a small counter with the sign: FLÈCHE TAXI FRANCE. The counter was deserted, but a man was locking a door directly behind it.

'M'sieu Montalbon?'

The man straightened, a pallid little man with grey hair, pale summer suit, and a pre-tied snap-on bow tie. And a frown. 'Closed for déjeuner,' he said. 'Come back in two hours.'

'But I am Leon Chambois,' Serault said. 'Of Zufall Productions.'

'Cham . . . ? Ah, about the Alouette. However, I was just –'

'It is fortunate that we're not too late. Allow me to introduce our studio's latest discovery, Lillie Lafayette – ' Jennica smiling vapidly – 'Dancourt, our unit manager – ' Ledoux nodding – 'Gaffer, our cinematographer – ' Talmas squinting without his glasses – 'who unfortunately does not speak any French. But perhaps, M'sieu Montalbon, you could speak English instead?'

Montalbon appeared affronted. 'If you insist.'

'It'd simplify matters. And of course and most importantly, our genius director, the great Erich von Beverstadt.'

'A fine film,' Kalenberg said, 'is always a Zufall.'

'Excuse us,' Serault continued, 'but traffic was delaying.'

'I understand.' Montalbon reluctantly unlocked the door.

85

'Not been such an influx here since the early forties, and then they'd the grace to keep to themselves. M'sieu! Careful with your whip.'

'A fly, I saw it on your jacket.' Kalenberg strode past, occupying the office. 'You will be our pilot today, nein?'

'I'm afraid I'm no longer –'

'A disappointment. I would have enjoyed you with us.'

'We've a fully qualified pilot I'm sure you'll approve. He speaks various languages.' Montalbon stopped behind his desk, dialling the airport operator and requesting a Fernand Roche be paged to report. Serault and Kalenberg sat in front of the desk, the others arranging themselves on a long couch across the small room, glancing idly at pictures of planes and an aerial survey map. Until Montalbon hung up and swivelled around in his chair, opening a drawer and sliding a contract printed in triplicate across his desk. He offered his pen and a smile of porcelain. 'The usual formalities. If one of you . . . ?'

Serault took the form and pen and began writing lies in the spaces indicated. Montalbon tented his fingers as if to do prayer, saying to Kalenberg: 'You're most fortunate. By the sheerest good luck we've a pilot and helicopter free.'

Kalenberg thrust forward. 'Free?'

'Ah, almost. There being a paltry deposit of 2,000 francs now, a 1,000 franc per diem rental fee, for a minimum of five days.'

'Outrageous.' Thwack went the crop down across the form.

'The height of our season, but for you a special rate. 900.'

'I filmed *Surge* at that. No deposit and 200 francs per day.'

An inner door opened and a young man entered. 'You rang, sir?'

'Yes, Fernand. Meet movie director von Beverstadt.' Then to Kalenberg: 'This is your pilot for 1,750 deposit and 825 for four days.'

'400 and 250 a day.'

'750 per but I insist on a week's minimum.'

'I want it for location work, not to start my own shuttle service. 750 it is, but 750 deposit and no minimum.'

'1,450 and Sundays off, my final offer.'

'Miss Lafayette was hired for less. A bit part admittedly, as the chirpy clerk in my *Liverpool Librarian*, caught in the stacks with Pops Shannon the grizzled custodian, daubing library paste on his – '

'1,000 now,' Serault interrupted. '500 per for three days.'

'Deal,' Montalbon said quickly.

Serault counted out the deposit as Kalenberg signed the form impressively and illegibly. Jennica abruptly stood and moved with a stripper's glide to the office door, holding it open and saying. 'I'll be off, since everything seems to be under control.'

Montalbon looked pained. 'Aren't you coming?'

'Oh but no. My tummy gets frightfully airsick.'

'Then stay for a sandwich. A drink.'

'How sweet of you to ask, Mr Montalbon. Anytime, some other time.' Tac tac of her high heels on the lobby floor and the undulation of her hips in their sockets. Leaving the door ajar and Montalbon's attention diverted. While Kalenberg wiped the contract free of fingerprints and prodded it over with his crop. 'There. Show us our machine and we won't detain you longer from your lunch.'

'Thoughtful, but Fernand can escort you from here.'

Roche was eyeing the franc notes. 'Sir, concerning my wages . . .'

'Later, boy.' Montalbon looking more pained.

'Yes, sir.' Roche looked more pained than Montalbon, and injured as if he'd heard later before. 'This way please, gentlemen.'

Through the inner door and along a narrow corridor. Roche short, natty in an iridescent green shirt, suede boots, and circling his chinos an embossed belt with a fist-sized silver buckle. Face round, flat-featured, fuzzy and freckled, topped with carroty hair pasted into meringue whirls, the entire effect giving his head an uncanny resemblance to Edam cheese. Ledoux behind, sizing Roche and suspicious of

87

country slickers who wear pants so tight they have to carry their wallet in a purse. Talmas followed, determined to keep a fatalistic and detached attitude towards the coming tribulation: if he learned to fly the copter, it would be memorable; if he did not . . . And with the thought a certain darkness once again came over his mind. Serault trailing, speaking low and clenched to Kalenberg:

'Stop slicing it so thick, Dieter, your part is padded enough.'

'Impossible, there's no such thing as a modest director. Or anybody else in cinema, or anybody on this decadent coast for that matter. Besides, there was a snide innuendo about Germans, and I saved us some money, didn't I?'

'Who cares how much or how long the rental is for?'

'The deposit, hozkapt. My depthfinder went to pay for it . . .'

They moved across tarmac seared by the sun, chain-link fence stretching on their right, the desert of a runway heat-shimmering left and centre. To a small quenset hangar, in front of which an Alouette III was parked, the emblem of an arrowhead entwined with F and T on its dusty hull. Squatting plump and bulbous on its skids, tail straight back and hooked with a tall vertical fin, like an angry if pregnant scorpion.

'Army surplus,' Roche said, approaching. 'An SE–316B using a 38 Artouste turbine.'

'Formidable.' Ledoux licking lips. 'How is the pickup?'

'Land in St Tropez and we'll be mobbed.'

'I meant the speed.'

'150 km/h. Gentlemen, will the craft satisfy?'

'Eminently,' Kalenberg said, taking one of the pairs of fine leather gloves Serault was distributing from his flight bag. 'Stop staring, Fernand, it's only a fetish of mine.'

Into the helicopter, which was not much different from the interior of a Volkswagen Microbus. Pilot up front over everything but the instrument panel, two passenger seats beside him and four behind, and stowage at the rear. Serault sitting behind Roche, making sure everyone had their gloves on. Talmas, next in row, retrieving his glasses from Ledoux and nervously rubbing an earlobe. Kalenberg managing to settle so it seemed he were behind everybody and being imperiously chauffeured, and Ledoux was across from Roche, studying how Roche ran through his preflight check. The squirt of exhaust, the whine of engine, the flapping vibrations of departure. Roche radioing the tower: ready for takeoff, VFR flight blah blah and the tower granting clearance. The helicopter sliding along, increasing speed and gently tilting, then gradually angling off the apron.

Serault leaned forward, yelling to Ledoux over the howl: 'I thought these things went right up in the air like a rocket.'

'Yes,' Ledoux shouting, 'if necessary. But it is safer to follow a height-velocity curve so a ratio of lift and – '

'Never mind.' Serault sinking back, exhausted from straining to hear what he couldn't understand.

Roche veered seaward towards the purple-shadowed Isles d'Hyères. Then called over his shoulder to Kalenberg: 'Sir? Where to, sir?'

'To the Riviera. Where I'm filming my next epic.'

Roche swung northeast, the direction of Nice, Monaco, and Menton. 'And sir, what will you be filming there?'

'*Crime and Punishment.*'

'The book? But it's Russian.'

'The magazine. I was undecided till I realized that with Hollywood at my foot I've a responsibility to be authentic. This must look more Russian than Russia, so instantly the Riviera sprang to mind.'

'I'll try to help, sir.'

Serault brought from his bag a bottle with a wedged cork and a small pencilled X. Unstoppered the bottle and offered it to Roche. 'Some Rouge? A Côte de Provence Carenzo does well.'

'No thanks.'

'Give it here,' Kalenberg said, and Serault took out a second bottle, superficially a twin, but without an X on the label and nitrazépam in the wine. 'Good for the heart,'

Kalenberg said, swallowing. 'Good for whatever ails you, especially flying.'

'That's just it,' Roche said. 'Do you have a coke or milk?'

'Ach, a Frenchman who doesn't imbibe his national debt?'

'I do, von Beverstadt sir, but not while on duty.'

Ledoux was a syrup of comrade and confidence: 'You've a point, Fernand. One shouldn't take too much of anything including wine, yet this is wine milder than grenadine and a sip would not be too much.'

Roche smiled, declining. 'But don't let me stop you.'

And Ledoux sat back, an alum line for a mouth.

Serault gazed out of the window again, despondent. Down at the deep ravines and eroded skyline of the Mauros Massif; at the dense covering of heaths where pine and oak had been decimated by fire; and rock had been burnt red as raw beef. . . . A stupid error that was, depending on this bottle. Yet I'd very few pills, and dividing them might've diluted their strength too much. And visiting the doctor for a prescription might have been a worse mistake: surely the police will be investigating afterwards, when our abstaining pilot is found. So perhaps it was less a blunder than a portent. A warning omen . . .

'Sir, I'm a great fan. I've seen all your films.'

'Fernand,' Kalenberg said, 'that wouldn't be difficult.'

'Sir, in your new film. Might there be an opening for me?'

'Perhaps, for a perceptive lad like yourself, though he'd have to be able to hold his liquor. A small but challenging walk-on.'

'I'll change my name to something rugged. To . . . Henri Thoreau.'

Talmas reacted: 'I think there was a writer by that name.'

'Writer,' Roche said. 'Who're writers compared to actors? Writers are failures, you sometimes wonder where they get their ideas. One performance by me and the hack will be forgotten.'

Ledoux urged. 'Why not try out for the part with the wine?'

'I shall. As soon as we land this evening.'

'Enthusiasm and creativity are spur of the moment,' Kalenberg said. 'This splendid chance won't be repeated later.'

'I could lose my licence, though. The laws are very strict.'

Serault recorked the bottle and crowned Roche with it.

Roche sighed, slumping forward in his belt harness. 'Not too suave,' Serault said, putting the bottle down. 'But he was going to take this wine one way or the other.'

The copter swayed gracefully in a mannered descent.

'Crash!' Kalenberg waved his arms. 'We're going to crash!'

'We won't fall out of the sky, Dieter.' Ledoux intense but not raising his voice. 'Even if the engine quits, auto-rotation will –'

'Never mind,' Serault said. 'Help get Roche back here.'

Ledoux unbuckled the pilot's belt, muttering serves him proper, look at his tapered shirt and crotchgrabber bell-bottoms, maybe you've knocked some sense into the peacock. Serault lifted out inert flesh, Kalenberg agitated but assisting. Talmas excused himself as he squeezed by to the front. Ledoux was at the helm, regaining altitude and waxing nostalgic about not having changed much except for the better and how this brings back the old days. That is wonderful Bernard, Kalenberg yelling, as long as it brings us tomorrow. Serault searched the flight bag for a roll of tape to bind the boy's ankles and wrists, and a velvet sack sewn by Jennica to fit over his head. Into the rear compartment with Roche, who was growing a goose-egg and groaning incoherently. Serault felt relieved no real damage had been done, and reminded the others not to use names, at least not their right ones. Roche about to awaken.

Ledoux was now explaining functions to Talmas, who kept nodding yes yes with a bleak oh Jesus expression. Remember your book lessons, Wesley: cyclic stick here controls tilt yes yes hence movement and direction. Collective pitch stick there controls angle of the main rotor blades yes yes thus the amount of lift. The throttle is this twist-grip on the collective, like a motorcycle handlebar, and the foot pedal varies the pitch of the tail. Yes yes. But do remember the pitch pedal is on the right and not on the left as in American craft, and here, you might as well take over, there is no more to show.

Oh Jesus.

Places were exchanged, the copter amazingly continuing to rotate and stay airborne. Talmas settled in the pilot's seat, leaden with trepidation, hitching his belt and wiping his hands on his trousers. He touched the cyclic stick. It swung easily, the copter banking lightly. Talmas glanced at Ledoux hunched between the seats beside him, and, encouraged, clutched both sticks. The copter wobbled, protesting. So were the men behind him.

'The cyclic,' Ledoux cried. 'Pull the stick, we'll level out.'

Stick. Which stick? Talmas pulled any stick with anxious haste, the copter making weird grating clatters. Talmas panicked, trying to compensate. The copter lurched, rising abruptly higher, then tilting violently and sliding sideways. Talmas released the collective stick and groped for his glasses which had fallen into his lap. 'I hit the air brakes,' he said. Mainly to himself, for Ledoux was no longer beside him.

Talmas twisted around, seeing his passengers thrashing about the deck. He forgot the pedal with a heavy foot. The copter was motionless for a brief instant, causing Talmas to lurch forward into the controls, causing a mechanical attempt at an intricate *pas seul*. There was a general scudding around and an impolite exchange of opinions, mostly in bellowed oaths. Ledoux tumbled, tripping Serault. Kalenberg kept a grip on the roll of tape while grappling for balance, the tape unreeling from the half-trussed Roche, clinging to and up-setting a bottle of wine. Roche, helpless in the scooping force of the drift, rammed into all of them. Serault clawed upright and hugged the upholstery, only to find himself engaged in a losing battle against a ski-slope terrain. He rolled with the tide of men, tape and wine, until he was brought up sharply against the glass of one window; through which was revealed a bombardier's direct view of the shoreline passing several thousand feet below. A waterfront complex of hotels and villas now, the Suquet Tower in Cannes, fountains throwing silver in Golfe-Juan villas, bathers hugging the bosom of Cap d'Antibes. Suddenly the sky again, crossed by scampering clouds, the transition so quick as to make it appear as a split-screen effect.

Absorbed with the sticks, Talmas was quaking. His forehead pasty white, little muscles standing out along his jaw like tack heads. A bottle rattling around beneath his foot, which he instinctively picked up, not wanting to be further irritated. Prying out the cork and taking a dram. A victim of circumstances, he was, and if anybody was entitled to a drink, it's a victim of circumstances. Yeah, this was a goddamn pisser, and the gentleman in black was riding copilot. Another noble swallow before the revolution.

Ledoux glassy-eyed, crawling, reached for the cyclic stick. Reckless from the jolt of wine and rotor, Talmas failed the rescue by whipping the copter into a tight parabola. The impact of the curve bowled away Ledoux, twisting the hull on its frame and almost pulling Talmas out of his seat. Everybody fell upon each other with audible noise, pungent wine spraying fast and loose and threatening blindness, feet to ear and teeth to arm in sprawly brotherhood among the coils of tape, annihilating the pleasantries of universal togetherness. Serault squashed flat and so full of torque his nose was dribbling; but I am not here, he mentally insisted . . . If the wine weren't a portent, this surely must be. What monster slipped me the notion of improving my lot? Who destroyed my static happiness with desire . . . ?

Nice was a blemish. Villefranche a hopeless blur. Talmas had the bottle tilted when skimming Monaco, and with a deep satisfied sigh he angled towards Roquebrune. 'Hey, I think I have this licked.'

'The hills,' Ledoux gasped from the jumble. 'Clear the hills.'

Talmas swizzled the sticks. 'Second floor, stockings sweaters lingerie.' Bellies plastering down over groins, stretching pops of bolts and crimps, the spine of hills separating Roquebrune from Menton sheared by a few metres.

'Third floor, handbags records books and perfume.' Over the crest and Talmas ploughed down the other side, guiding with flush-faced audacity. 'Fourth floor, knitwear giftware silverware and nowhere but Bernard's junk shoppe on the starboard. Face front please ladies, watch your step.'

The Monastère de l'Annonciade, gone in a smudge. Talmas banking, following the road. The large brown-roofed garage came into focus, Ledoux staggering forwards in a crumpled state, wheezing: 'I made a pad beside the crane. Touch down there. And you're low, Wesley, much too low. Lift up. Lift up.'

'Aye aye, sir. The good ship Expectorate about to dock.'

'Oyez!'

Buzzing into the car yard, the skids clipping the wooden fence, which burst with a rasp and went flat as far as they could see. Radio antennae snapping, a harvest of metal chaff. Talmas pulling back the cyclic stick, cutting the throttle and raising the collective. An agonized scream from the turbine, then nothing. The copter dropped the last few metres relatively slowly, landing with a jaw-clicking bump next to the crane and flattening the water tap. Talmas flipped switches, his voice slurring:

'All out. Transfer point for Anaheim, Azusa and Cucamunga.'

Before the blades had stopped turning, they were out and down in the bowl of dust. 'Gott, give me air.' Kalenberg on his knees. 'I almost was sick.'

Serault followed, tape sticking, sweat and wine soaking his clothes. 'Wesley T. You are a drunken bastard.'

'Wwe could have bbeen killed.' Ledoux enraged to a stammer, shaking his fist at the copter. 'Why didn't you listen to my instructions? Look at my fence, will you, it could have bbeen us.'

'Yeah.' Talmas leaned out of the open doorway, extending to all a bedazzled wink . . . then gradually sagging, gently folding, falling to sprawl on the dirt. Face down and snoring. The bottle beside him tipped to show a label with an X on it.

Chapter Twelve

'Going to your yard seemed a good idea at the time.'

'At one time all of this must have seemed a good idea.'

'Yesterday I'd my doubts too, but we're well under way now.' Starched, studded and linked in his tuxedo, Serault crossed the Place du Casino.

'We should've flown directly to the quarry.' Ledoux was unwilling to forgive or forget the previous afternoon: again without moustache and now vaguely resembling Henri Vattier, the way Henri would look when made up later on; and greatly resembling a beetle in his custom-tailored tails. 'That is, *I* should have. Dropping off you, Dieter, and Roche, and then and only then teaching Wesley to fly.'

'Wesley – he's fully recovered and waiting?'

'Yes, though for a while I thought he'd died.'

'I imagine he wished to when he awoke.'

'Twelve hours out, as many litres of coffee to revive him, and as many stone of my solicitous wife after she returned from her sister's. Swift of Dieter, thinking to tell Fifine that Wesley had contracted Asian flu while filming a Kung Fu movie. She was impressed, liking as she does to do things with her hands. But if you hadn't driven Roche to the quarry before she arrived, there'd have been no today. By the way, how's your budding Adonis?'

'Unmoved and uncomfortable, according to Marc. He phoned just before Jennica and I left the house, reporting the trucks are in place and they're heading back here. Damned if I see why you're so down on Roche. He's young is all; try to bridge the generation gap.'

95

'This is the first generation which considers a gap unnecessary to keep the brats at bay. Besides, gap hell. Any boy with spangled pants and whorled hair is prowling for whatever he can get.'

'The passion of us all ...'

Alongside the casino, rigid against a full moon sky, Serault and Ledoux pressed through crowds, and where there were crowds there were police. Cruisers roaming slowly in fixed geometric patterns, lines of uniformed patrolmen rhythmic with the tide of sightseers, watching the crowds and the crowds watching the arrivals. The nobles from New Jersey and elsewhere. Alighting from limousines, flashing smiles of good dentistry and tickets of fine engraving at guards stationed by the terrace entrance. Breezing by an inconspicuous physiognomist doodling shrewdly on a pad. Who did not recognize Ledoux and drew notations so he would again, but who remembered Serault from years before and classified accordingly, with indifference ...

The Red Cross Gala is the most extravagant display of distinguished society in the world. You can barely imagine the fame accorded those chosen for the Princess's personal invitation list, and the intrigue that goes on to obtain a nearby table. This year the spectacle was held at the Casino, the terrace facing the sea swathed in over two miles of muslin, brocade and tulle fishnet. A pink sweetness seemingly sprinkled with stars fallen from heavens above as if in blessing. A giant clamshell was elevated against the Casino wall, on which André Rasseaux enchanted the privileged with his bewitching violin orchestra, and where beneath was arranged a wonderful fantasy of fireworks with which to draw the ostentatious evening to a close. All this romantic atmosphere was enhanced by 500 candles set in bouquets of waterlilies. Valets flanked the flower-covered arches and dancing pathes, their jackets and knee-britches bright scarlet and their stockings and wigs snowy white. In the excitement and glamour of the occasion, I tended to forget mundane earthly realities ...

Down the wide flight of steps beside the lighted flowerbeds, Serault feeling ambivalent about the physiognomist, relieved and yet slightly miffed to be pigeon-holed and dis-

96

missed so easily. To the decorated terrace below, Ledoux adjusting his butterfly tie and asking: 'Are Jennica and Dieter here?'

'Somewhere in this froth. Though we're keeping apart to avoid any whisper of collusion. The same should apply to you.'

'I've so much make-up on, they'd have to chisel through to my identity. You'll be safe for the few minutes I'll be here making my Appearance. However, I warn you you risk catching a cold.'

'You do sound more nasal. I assumed it was part of your act.'

'No, I think I caught one from all the water colours I've been spraying. The price of perfection. The ambulance looks quite authentic. I took a massive dose of penicillin so the basic infection as well as my sinusitus is more or less beaten back.'

'Then have a drink. It'll pick up your pace and spirits too.'

'Can we afford it?'

Said snidely: Serault ignored the tone. 'We're broke, but we've managed to cut the tickets we need from six to four, so a drink for you isn't unreasonable. Now, you've Wesley's key, haven't you?'

'Yes. And I won't forget to take the passage to the Hôtel, or leave the tickets when I change, or hide the key in the hall before returning to the garage. Don't nag. I know the sequence of events.'

'Two drinks for you. The second to add sport.'

'Ah, you're right. I'm becoming querulous from strain.' Ledoux glanced at the limpid sky. 'Hardly any cover, is there?'

'Darkness won't make any difference. And according to superstition, a full moon encourages submission and other forms of insanity.'

'Nothing superstitious about it, René. It's the only rational explanation for our presence here . . .'

This is the 'show-off' capital of the world, pure-blooded princes

97

and movie queens mingling with financial magnates and business kings. Baron Gelien; Colonel Harrison Grey Otis the Equadorian cattle tycoon; 'Bow-wow' Davenport; Dublin Dan Liston who flew in from his Broadway hit show; Lemon Jefferson who came with his valet – and I could list another hundred personages equally famous – were on hand at this exclusive club of clothes and jewels. From Princess Fazenda; Madame Bedingford and her Daughter; the Duchess Califia, world hang-glider champion Mary Doss; to the American star Polly Ellen Pop; Lady Sylvia Davis and the artist Naromji – all dressed to the teeth. Several women totalled more than a million dollars in carats each. And during this annual event which fulfils all dreams, flashbulbs popped and cameras were recording it for posterity . . .

Serault wedged his way across the terrace sacchrin beneath the moon. Among those shiny men without bloat or pallor, under tan control through golf and preferences for Swedish exercises. Hearty after a year of reduced capital and increased taxation, shaking hands, patting backs, measuring where to stab. Born with silver knives. And those wives the colour and texture of dried jerky, either angular from enforced starvation or plump in low décolletage, breasts aquiver like puddings. And those wives between husbands, introducing current Good Friends of rippling muscle and dimpling chin, bred for impeccable comportment and instant erection. And those studs between wives, escorting those supple beauties between affairs, of thighs that spread never pucker, bedroom larvae chewing holes in these shiny men. And Serault unable to differentiate the one breathlessly nearing from the one chittering behind from the one in the dress of embroidered diamanté beads at a price she daren't even whisper. Seeing instead Kalenberg, belly sucked in and chest stretching seams, approaching with oddly mincing steps. Ignoring instructions with a blithe smile, a disturbing precedent.

'René. If publicity and jet lag don't fell the average playboy, this gala will. I'm impressed, having been a failure for so long.'

'Has your corset affected your brain? Get away from me.'

'This girdle is killing me. But don't get excited, I'm moving on, I only want to clarify a detail. When do I leave and how?'

'Sometime very shortly after the dancing starts. I doubt it matters what excuse you give as long as it's logical.'

'Then I shall sup vintage wine from some lady's slipper and use the pretext of accidentally choking on her hidden corn plaster.'

'Considering our future is riding on the present, Dieter, I'd hoped you'd behave with greater restraint and propriety.'

'A fine one to complain, René. Not a shred of either in you and now I understand. Something very narcotic about this scene. We could do worse than to meet this evening on its own terms . . .'

When their Royal Highnesses entered onto the staircase of the magnificent terrace, the guests greeted them with loud admiration and praise. Prince Rainier III looked every inch the reigning monarch he is. Princess Grace and her daughter had chosen the same famous couturier, Christian Dior. The mother wore a long gown in yellow organdy imprinted with orange peonies; her hair was styled in a braided twist by Alexandre. She had a crown of diamonds, drop diamond earrings, and an emerald and diamond necklace. Caroline, her hair shorter and curled, wore a feather-stitched aster print with halter neckline and bare back. The charming young princess had the poise of a Cinderella as she stood between her parents, and, in my opinion, the sight was well worth the price of the invitation. Their entrance prolonged by greedy photographers, the First Family of Monaco moved statelily towards their table to the sound of enthusiastic applause . . .

The opulence smothered Serault, aggravating his old resentments. He was back in the social cauldron and yet out of it. Forced out, barred by exchanges of civil pleasantries which never quite became friendly overtures.

Serault glimpsed Jennica near the balcony, a samurai in a breastplate of silk chiffon and paste diamonds. He angled the opposite way, not wanting to confront her effervescence, her candy eyes, and have to think of wise and penetrating comments laced with familiar gentle humour . . .

'René, you have some nerve.'

Serault turned, startled: to be pierced by Nicole Hibou's breasts, rapiers in a black velvet dress. Mountings for a dazzling if unfamiliar necklace. Leaner nose and thinner lips than he remembered, though they could be for tonight's indignation. His fraudulent greeting was nipped in the preamble. 'Why how nice – '

'Showing yourself after what you did to me last Christmas.'

'You must be mistaking me for – '

'I dare say. Fairly smacks of your wormy imagination, placing that subscription to *Swapper's Guide* in my name, and the classified advertisement too. "Iron maiden with trapeze desires discipline by soccer team." You've no idea what filthy replies I received. I've never been so insulted and degraded in my whole life.'

'Glad to hear it, it might do you good.'

'My lawyer said I'd at least a nuisance case, and if you weren't so insolvent, I'd have sued. But I thought of a more fitting way to teach you your lesson. Do you like my necklace?'

'Pleasant; not as imposing as mine.'

'It is yours.'

'Nicole. What have you done?'

'I had it reset.' She edged towards a palm as if desiring something between them. 'The stone had to be shaved to 12 carats 65 points but just everybody agrees it's much more stylish. Don't you?'

Serault's half-lidded eyes calculated the length of rope required to replace the necklace. Deceptively calm. 'Ah Nicole. So many letters to choose from – how was your teamwork?'

She stiffened, her expression implacable. To draw abruptly away, leaving a wake of hostility behind her . . .

During the dinner of haute cuisine, the special attractions on stage were presented. Chanteuse Rabin Sequine, winner of the prestigious European songfest, appeared in a see-through bosom save for some pointilliste glitter, and delighted the audience with her songs. Then came an advance presentation of Cirque's autumn-winter collection of draped crepes and furs with uneven

100

hemlines. The spectators then viewed the suspense-filled drawing of the richly endowed lottery ...

Serault sat at his assigned table, far to one side and back where Moroccan busboys were swatting flies with their trays. His circle of unillustrious diners had been chosen to encourage his insanity, having money up to their ears and nothing inbetween. Prichard of the hairy nose and fingers yellowed from cigars, an expense-paid congressman married to a woman with wens under her eyes, a ginger fright wig, and a diamond solitaire the size of a peach stone. Wivell of the boiled collar and neck, whose father had done everything so he did nothing, except believe in the occult and the re-emergence of the Empire. His tubby wife wearing an armlet once owned by the Doges of Venice. Karaguez, a septuagenarian, his latest bride of eighteen smelling puffy of bed and unable to hold her head straight for the weight of her ear-rings, a wedding present. And because Serault was ostensibly alone, he'd been paired with Madame Delasparre, a pale widow subject to vapours, her chief attraction a 700 carat topaz in a Braque-designed setting. Dressed in ruffles, pink flowers in her hair, she perfectly matched the decor.

Serault keeping to himself, finding himself rather blocked by the smarm of conversation and the mush-footed serving of courses. The consommé en gelée – Africa was thrilling, we visited every Hilton there. The lobster mousse – Monet, Picasso; I may not know art, but for investment I know what I like. The eternal chicken garnished with fiddled-up vegetables – We all favour a classless society, dear, providing it has proper leadership. The pièce montée capable of warping dentures – One must be concerned with the quality of life; M'sieu Serault, you've barely spoken, but don't you agree one has a duty to ecology?

'Indeed so, Madame, and if in one's garden there's a marble fireplace with a mirror where it's grate was, one's party guests are inhibited from peeing on one's bougain-villea.'

Gazing around abstractedly, Serault spotted Kalenberg a

few tables distant holding court with some ladies of not more than one face-lift per. Serault declined the waiter's genteel hint to buy a cigar, apprehensively watching Kalenberg. Who continued in the manner of an eccentric gentleman of independent means known to be a good tipper. Candlelight puddling through crystal. Coffee congealing in china thimbles. Kalenberg reaching decisively for the plate of petite fours. Stopping in mid-stroke with stricken look. His shirt rupturing from over-exertion, catapulting studs and expanding from collar to cummerbund. To display proudly the trademark of the Mainstay Corset Company underneath. A spouting whale. Excusing himself, napkin clasped to his chest, flaming chagrin. Dieter was a bit early and disorganized, Serault thought. But on the whole, a rather unique and convincing reason to leave the gala . . .

It was after midnight when the second great highlight of the evening took place. Prince Rainier opened the ball escorting his daughter onto the elevated dance floor for the first dance. Soon Princess Grace joined them with Prince Polignac, Rainier's uncle. Then everybody was dancing, the women in their summery gowns looking like pastel ghosts under the warm moonlight. When they were not dancing, the guests had their choice of refreshments at their tables, the intimate atmosphere of the Black Jack Club, or gambling upstairs in the renowned salons of the Casino itself . . .

The table temporarily vacant except for Serault. And a waiter determined to pour his champagne, though so far thwarted. Each time he'd try, Serault dipped into the ice-bucket first and sprinkled a bare minimum into his glass. The only method of milking one bottle to last the length of the dinner. The waiter was sulking nearby, Serault anticipating another attempt, when Jennica suddenly sat down in Madame Delasparre's chair.

'I saw Dieter leave in something of a rout.'

'First him,' Serault said. 'Now you.'

'So I think I'll be on my way to the room.'

'I appreciate being notified, but we weren't to meet.'

'You and that Nicole weren't to meet either.'

'Oh Christ. I had no choice, Jennica, she trapped me.'

'Using your necklace as bait, I suppose.'

'I want nothing to do with her, I swear it. Nicole is a cosmopolitan small *c* girl, conceited, manipulative, with occasional lunges of sexuality. Nicole was a mistake. Please, I dearly wish to forget her.'

'V'la,' the waiter murmured, topping the glass with the last of the champagne while Serault's attention was diverted. Departing with bottle and bucket, satisfied with a technical knock-out. Jennica glancing at him, saying vaguely, 'Is this . . . all there is?'

'Yes. Drink it if you want it, I'm not thirsty.'

'I mean the gala. Oh I knew you told me so, yet still it's a bit of a disappointment. Really no more than a cocktail party.'

'A bar whimsy. A fraud created by mechanics and technology. But this is fact as opposed to public relations, so don't despair or consider yourself singular. Come to think of it, all any resort can offer are brief flashes of self-delusion, but that's another issue we'll not explore tonight. Ah, Madame Delesparre is coming . . .'

Serault watched Jennica fading among the guests, listened to the orchestra fretting and whining above the slippery hum of dancers, none too old or dignified to glide phantasmal in the moonlight. Another ten minutes, then Serault went into the Black Jack Club, entering the old-fashioned lift leading to the Salles Privés. Taking the long way around to reach the Hôtel passage, the Prince's private staircase having been opened tonight for general use. Unnecessary and not part of any plan. Merely a nostalgic desire to relive the abandoned experience before he changed it and himself beyond recognition.

Once again stepping from the grilled cage, into a thick florid marsh. Of heavy oak walls and floral carpet, curls of smoke and ruddy players under low-slung lamps, the croupiers' chants of *messieurs, faites vos jeux*. Through swing doors into the stuttering swamp of blackjack and craps; of *Deux as* – snake eyes – and *scarpette nueve* – baby

103

needs new shoes. Into the stained glass and muralled ocean of The Kitchen; of the green baize tables of trente-et-quarante, and Dostoievsky's roulette wheels which have neither memory nor conscience. Normally bustling as a train depot and appealing to the same clientele, but tonight mostly deserted, the casino closed to those without tickets. And those at the gala preferring the Salons Privés, having more to lose.

Now out into the entrance hall, feeling a growing excitement and anticipation. Accepting it reluctantly as he walked towards the cloakroom entrance, passing various guards and pausing for the passage lift. The dark cynicism inside Serault carping at him that he was without redemption, sneering there is no proof

that Van Gogh painted any better
by slicing off
his ear.

Chapter Thirteen

Serault sat in his underwear at the vanity table.

The welt of a nylon stocking covered his hair, matting it down so Jennica could roll a tawny wig over him, adjusting and spraying it, patting it in place. Then she took putty to thicken and protrude his ears and fill in the bridge of his nose, painting the putty's join lines with flexible collodion. A dark-blonde grease-paint stick brushed his eyebrows against their normal direction, colouring them, making them shaggy and overhanging. Tending to sink his eyes. In the mirror, Serault watched Jennica work, then glanced at the reflections of Kalenberg and the Vattiers nearby.

They watched in return with a certain malicious amusement, having already gone through their ordeals, Marc tilting back in a chair, his wig iron-grey, his face now sallow and broken-nosed with a slightly pained expression: due to the tightness of his beige guard's uniform and his elevator shoes wedged to cause pigeon-toeing. Henri, lounging on the bed, was also pale, more of an office pallor. He wore Ledoux's bow tie and tuxedo, the basted cuffs of which were lowered to fit his longer frame. The tails were tucked in his trousers and a regular jacket on over it, giving the effect of a standard business suit. Shading at the corners of his mouth and eyes, shadows about his Adam's apple, whitener streaking the temples of his restyled hair – he was a decade older and dissipating by the year. Kalenberg sat on the other edge of the bed, his features narrower, ears flattened and lips thinner. He wore horn-rimmed tinted glasses, a boot-black Valentine wig, and a different, more distinctive tuxedo.

Jennica swivelled Serault around, applying spirit gum where his Van Dyke would go, and paused to let the gum set. Serault eyed the three men, saying: 'Seeing how you look cheers me no end. It makes suffering these indignities infinitely easier.'

'Ugliness hurts,' Marc said.

'It also gives me confidence for tonight as I've confidence for little else.' His voice had an almost Bogart husk to it, sponge rubber balls in his mouth thickening his speech while reducing the prominence of his cheekbones. 'Dieter, you and Bernard are unknown and under assumed names. Marc and Henri, you're not connected with the gala at all. And Jennica, the unfortunate, anonymous blonde of this fray, has done our disguises so well nobody will know us.'

'Except you, René,' Jennica said. 'They might recognize you.'

'Only in the way people are recognized at school reunions, as faint parodies of themselves. Besides, I'll use the mask later.'

Kalenberg turned to the Vattiers. 'I think René is giving us what Wesley would term a locker-room pep talk.'

'Dieter, that's unfair. I'm not one for false much less genuine complacency, but I truly believe – '

'Oh hush,' Jennica cut in tersely. 'Let me put the beard on.'

Quickly and efficiently she attached the Van Dyke using preformed strips of yak hair. First along Serault's underchin, then along the sides from his hairline down, then the front section and the moustache. Finally, with pan-stik make-up and a damp sponge she darkened his skin to a 'tourist' tan, highlighting and shadowing, smoothing upwards and outwards to add to his air of square Teutonic fleshiness. She critically surveyed, trimmed a few hairs, and stood back again. 'Yes . . . Your jawline is entirely changed now.'

Serault surveyed his image in the glass. 'Chérie, you're an artist.'

'How thrilling. Now go and get dressed.'

'An artist by trade,' he told her, 'but a born nanny.' Up from the vanity and across Talmas's hotel room. To the foyer, where in the cupboard were two black satchels; the attaché case; and the collapsible frame, folded and propped against the wall like an ornate pair of skis. Hanging were Serault's new outfit and Kalenberg's old tuxedo, complete with Talmas's size and label should it be checked.

Jennica had a small overnight suitcase, which she was packing with her make-up materials and Serault's tuxedo. Serault dressed in the same white shirt, a striped tie, and a blue serge suit cunningly sewn with darts and pads to alter his build. He walked back in plain oxfords, an oddly splay-footed stride. 'Dashing, eh?'

'What you need,' Henri said, 'is an eyepatch.'

'One over each eye,' Kalenberg added.

'How *can* you.' Jennica rapped the suitcase shut with belligerency. 'There's enough things in this case to blow up the entire hotel. How can you crack jokes at a time like this?'

'Because we're afraid,' Serault replied gently. 'It's natural and inevitable or we'd be bigger fools than we probably are already.'

She hugged herself as if cold. 'You don't have to do it.'

'Ah, but we do.'

'René . . . is this kill or be killed?'

'Chérie, human lives aren't part of our game.'

'This is no game.'

'It is, and with rules.'

Jennica pointed towards the curtained window, her mouth pink and quivering like the underlip of a calf. '*They* don't have rules. And if they did, they'd not give a bloody damn about keeping them.'

'They do. The rules are called precautions or contingency plans or whatever, and they have to follow them. Too many innocent bystanders not to. Our game is merely based on upsetting their own rules.' Serault placed an arm around her shoulder. 'You just wait and see.'

She nodded dully, almost forlornly, pulling away to carry

the suitcase into the foyer. 'I'd better get back to the gala.'

Serault asked her, 'Your tone-call's all set?'

Another nod, opening the hall door. 'But I'm not sure when . . .'

'Don't worry, you'll know when. The air becomes electric, everybody tensing and craning their necks. But you hold off until the Family actually gets up and starts shaking hands. That'll give us just about the right amount of time.'

'Very well.' She stood on the threshold for a moment, fingering her tiny beaded purse. 'I . . . I'm sorry I snapped just now, René. And also the way I acted back at the dinner, too. Please . . .'

Serault held up a hand. 'Don't. Don't say it, don't say be careful. Monaco is enough of a cliché as it is.'

She smiled a rigid smile and shut the door behind her. No sound of her footsteps, the hallway carpet swallowing with a hush.

Serault sat back down at the dressing table. Propping his chin in his hands. Subsiding as the other three were, subdued and waiting for her signal. Yet feeling singularly puzzled by her reactions . . . For all her avidity, she'd expressed disappointment in the gala and qualms about the heist and their safety. Steps forward, and sounding genuine enough. What with one thing and another, she'll likely catch up with herself and become a splendid wife, mother, and adult. I doubt I'll know her after this is all over. A sadness, but nothing much to be done about it . . .

Ledoux waited for his own signal. The explosions themselves.

Hunched on a stool in the rented garage. Trying to ignore the irritating light, which was a bare lamp bulb swinging on its cord in small eccentric circles, making him dizzy and casting shadows on the Citroën. René's wagon was repainted an eggshell white, red crosses on the front doors and tail gate, and frosting on its side and rear windows. A luggage rack had been clamped to the roof, holding a blue revolving flasher and sign panels reading ASSURANCE AMBULANCE SERVICE. Along the back wall was a bench cluttered with tools, wood and wire, odd parts, and brushes. On the sloping concrete floor were cans of paint, boxes of soap, a portable electric sprayer, and a couple of mops with damp coloured heads. A hose ran across the floor and through a chink in the alleyway door, around to a tap by the stairs to the flat above.

Ledoux, shoulders slumped, wiped dust and bits of plaster from his intern's smock, listening to the sounds of violence working through the ceiling. The Kasetzakers were arguing again. Ledoux couldn't tell what about, most of the specific charges muffled, but he knew from long experience with Fifine that the accusations didn't really matter. It was the principle of the thing.

An E-string shrillness long and shrivelling, coupled with a basso profano. Sometimes separate verses, sometimes as a duet, advancing and retreating across the floor above, interspersed with furniture dull and heavy or crockery accenting staccato. Massed with a choir of four children. Converging for the moment over the large drainpipe which ran down one side of the garage – a barricade in the bathroom, which Ledoux had come to discover was the family sanctuary. Not this time, evidently. A squawk, and immediately afterwards a crunch, rattling the pipe. A second squawk, the slam of a door, the shouting dying down.

Peace, Ledoux thought, eyes heavenward. Catching sight of a drop of water oozing out from between the planks. The drop growing, sidling along the ceiling which like a bed was bowed in the middle. The drop hesitated, then fell on the hood of the Citroën. Ledoux held his breath, disbelieving. Another drop slowly filtered through the cracks, and now Ledoux was off the stool, running towards the car, snatching up a bucket to catch the leak.

Upstairs, one of the Kasetzakers flushed the toilet.

Ledoux was leaning awkwardly, bucket held up in hope, when the solid sheet of water poured from above. A sudden torrential monsoon, drenching him and spewing across the fresh paint, washing it away, ceasing as quickly as it'd begun.

'Christ and his unfortunate Father!' Ledoux left the bucket on the hood to catch a few worthless dribbles. Out of the garage, and up the stairs two at a time. To thump on the Kasetzakers' door.

M'sieu Kasetzaker opened the door, light spilling out on the stoop from a flat much like himself. Unimaginative and drab, a place of bed-wetting and gas rings. He with a wary glint in his eye, a thick brown moustache, and a shirt of sour armpits. Exhausted from working all day to come home to this. One hand still buckling his belt. 'Eh?'

'You've sprung a leak!' Ledoux said frantically.

'Eh?'

'A leak! Stop, you're flooding out the garage! Don't you understand? You're ruining me – ah, the drain is broken and water is pouring through. Whatever you do, don't use the bathroom.'

Kasetzaker digesting, turning to shout at a closed door: 'Brigitte? The man from downstairs, he says – '

'Don't yell at me. Can't I have peace even in here?'

Ledoux clung to the jamb. 'She isn't – '

A flushing of the toilet.

'Oyez!' Leaping back down the stairs, into the garage again to see the ravages of the second flood. Because the planks were laid diagonally across the joists, the water had showered on an angle, scrubbing the Citroën clean from left front fender to right rear bumper. Slantwise, the car was effectively half white, half tea-rose pink. He could hurriedly respray, Ledoux supposed – he'd have to, the original pink too dangerous to leave exposed and risk being traced later. But he was out of white paint. The only tempra left in sufficient quantity was a chocolate brown he'd used to camouflage the helicopter. Brown was simply out of the question . . . yet when it came down to basics, there wasn't any question to be asked.

Galvanized with desperation, Ledoux grabbed all the dry rags and chamois off the bench, and began rubbing dry the section he'd have to repaint. Praying he had enough time. And that the Kasetzaker children wouldn't need to go potty . . .

Wesley T. was also waiting.

Sitting on the running board of the junk yard crane, a few metres from the helicopter. The copter checked, warmed, resting ready to go; Wesley not ready to go, his head throbbing from the lingering effects of the doctored wine. Jesus, this was a distressing period. A month ago he couldn't manage a decent wet dream, and here he now was embroiled in major crime, the same diffident dyspeptic self he'd always been. Was this paradox the way it had to be – and if so, why couldn't it have occurred when he was young, bursting with enthusiasm and barren of experience? Next thing he'd know, he'd be wanting to eat meat . . .

Gazing idly about as if for relief: at the house across the yard, where two windows upstairs were bright, Madame Ledoux stalking back and forth upon occasion. But not for the moment. Then he searched the dark acreage of rusted cars, assuring himself there was nothing out there. Hiding. Lurking. No sounds, no sounds at all. Talmas was straining to catch the slightest noise, his mind wandering feebly with fears and strange fancies . . .

Sounds. A creak of door, the simpering of a giggle.

Talmas stood. 'Who's there?'

'Little me. I couldn't sleep.' Madame Ledoux rolled towards him from the downstairs barn, gold teeth glinting in the moonlight. One hand daintily lifting the full skirt of her baby-blue peignoir. Of gigantic folds, a Bedouin tent with fluffy buttons like guinea pigs crawling up her front. 'I thought you might be lonely, too.'

'Jesus.' Talmas unnerved, stunned motionless as she swept near.

'Don't be shy, dear man. We're alone but we're adults.'

'No, I . . . I heard something else, Mrs Ledoux. Didn't you?'

'Call me Fifine.'

Talmas peered wildly around. 'Definitely something else.'

'Only cats. We've lots of cats to catch the mice.' A wink and a nudge of elbow. Talmas sat down abruptly. Madame joined him on the board, the crane listing with protesting springs. 'No reason to be worried about some cats and mice. No reason at all.'

But Talmas was worried about the way she plucked at her buttons, and pretended not to notice her negligée hitching over hippo knees.

She seemed to sense his aversion and fright, tweaking his cheek coyly between thumb and forefinger. 'Why, what a strange look you have in your eye. What's the matter? I'm not going to eat you.'

Madame Ledoux didn't add the word they were both thinking:

Yet.

Chapter Fourteen

The attaché case chimed.

Jennica ringing on schedule, Serault hoped, though there wasn't any particular timetable other than that of logic and predictability. No need to issue orders – the men responding by rote, clearing Talmas's room and moving down the hall to the lift, descending to the corridor left of the main desk, there to pause warily with their equipment and anxieties.

The vast lobby was a sinking ship. The few remaining guests deserting it to thrust outside, clotting with others in the Place du Casino and along Avenue de Monte-Carlo. Anticipating the departure of the Rainiers. How they could tell it was imminent mystified Serault, but they knew. Somehow they always intuited such events, clotting together at appointed times with their tongues of clatter and faces of fromage. And Serault, stretching the fingers of his thin pigskin gloves, felt strangely pacified by this phenomenon: sensing obscurely that it, along with his own plans, seemed to be following some preordained pattern.

The American Bar closed. One lonely bellhop still in his teens was over by the windows staring out at the crowds. The Horsten display guard dozed after too many years of too many galas. Only two other employees, behind the main desk and dressed remarkably similarly to Henri and Serault in dark serge suits: the concierge leafing through papers by the cashier's cage, simulating activity for the benefit of the manager. The manager trying disdainfully to get rid of a short, ruddy drunk clad in orange trousers and an aloha shirt.

The drunk was now the single guest in the lobby. Serault didn't like the idea of a customer being present, but then, nobody else seemed to either. Serault decided to chance it anyway. A quick nod: Henri idled across the lobby towards the bellhop. Kalenberg strolled past the desk to the opposite corridor and the men's room. Marc rested the doorframe against a pillar and walked to the Horsten guard, leaving Serault to cover the desk.

Marc approaching. The guard tilting his head, recognizing the uniform if not the face, and hoping to exchange a few common sighs and complaints from one in harness to another. But Marc acting as if to pass wordlessly, and it wasn't until he was alongside the guard that he suddenly struck an agonized expression, grunting.

The guard jumped up, catching Marc. 'What is it?'

'Oh my kidneys.' Marc gripping his side, doubling over.

'Here, sit down. I'll fetch help, a doctor.'

'No . . . to the bathroom, is all. I'm clogged to the brim.'

'But I can't. I can't leave my post.'

Henri now in a flank attack, snapping fingers at the bellhop. 'Boy,' he said. 'You, see to this man. We're not paying you to gawk at passerbys.'

'Sir.' The bellhop saluting, trotting to Marc. But when he tried bracing Marc by one shoulder, Marc leaned on so much weight his legs buckled. Marc turned imploring eyes to the guard. 'Ohh help me, brother,' he moaned anew.

The guard looked wretched, torn between duty, fraternity, and impending catastrophe. Henri with a haughty sniff imported the opinion that the immediate threat to the carpet was greater than any to the display. Reluctantly, the guard took Marc's other shoulder, staggering as he and the bellhop propelled Marc to the men's room.

The manager was still buttonholed by the drunk and noticed nothing except his unsavoury breath. The concierge, more curious than concerned, lowered his papers and craned his neck. Serault came up to the counter and dropped one of his satchels on the counter.

'Do you mind. A little service here, please.'

114

'Oh.' The concierge coming over, attention diverted. 'Sorry, Sir, I'm afraid I didn't see you there. What can I do for you?'

'I was wondering about your safety deposit drawers . . .'

The bellhop opened the men's room door and the trio shunted inside: where Kalenberg was lurking with gun in hand. Marc straightened, gripping both men around the neck. The gun digging into the guard's flabby side, Kalenberg said: 'Don't move.'

'I can't move,' the guard wheezed, chin high and eyes large.

Kalenberg removed an old Le Français 7.65mm revolver from the guard's holster. 'Don't move,' he said again, unsure of what to say. Stepping back apace. 'Don't move and you won't get hurt.'

The bellhop was a disbeliever. He stomped hard on Marc's instep and squirmed free from the choking hold as Marc clenched his teeth. Lunging for one of the pistols while Kalenberg and the guard stood bewildered, the old revolver being fumbled and accidentally dropping into the latrine. At Marc's feet. The bellhop crawling frantically for it, to be kicked on the side of the head by Marc and rolling over.

The guard, stationary, looked at the boy and rubbed his neck. Kalenberg fished out the pistol and Marc dragged the boy into a closet stall, yanked down the uniform pants and propped the boy on the seat. 'You do the same,' he called out to the guard.

The guard shrugged, unbuckled and sat down in the adjoining stall. Waiting placidly while Marc stuffed a plain cotton handkerchief into the bellhop's mouth, then wrapped it, him, the tank and the bowl into a solid package. Cutting the reinforced tape with a pocket knife, locking the stall door and crawling out from underneath.

'Where're the keys?' Marc asked the guard.

'For the display? The desk has them, probably the manager. Not me.'

'I don't want to have to come back.'

'The young are rash,' the guard said. 'Me, I've been

115

around long enough to be smart about these things. Search me if you like.'

'No.' Marc took another handkerchief, rolling it into a rope.

'Only key I've got is the one for my scooter,' the guard said.

'I'll make it easy on you, so you won't choke.' Marc gagged the guard, who nodded his appreciation. Marc paused. 'But we're going to be around a while making some noise. For your own good, don't you make any.' The guard shook his head earnestly as Marc taped him to the toilet. Again he locked the door and wormed his way out from underneath the stall.

Kalenberg had hidden the wet pistol in the waste paper basket and was standing by the door wiping his gloves with a towel. Marc, joining him, looked back at the knobby knees and pants at half mast, and thought with satisfaction that their prisoners looked well occupied...

Serault, procrastinating, was talking rubbish with the concierge. Paused as he saw Marc and Kalenberg emerge from the men's room and walk to where Henri was standing at the lobby portal. They trooped towards the desk. The drunk had now gone and the manager was filing his nails. 'Yes, I think you should take it,' Serault now said, extending the satchel by its handle. The concierge automatically reached for it by its sides, saying: 'We'll take good care of it.'

Serault said pleasantly, 'If you let go, I'll shoot you.'

The concierge blinked. 'Sir, I don't understand.'

'Look.' Serault with his other hand levelled his automatic: on the counter beside the satchel where only the concierge could see it pointing centimetres from his chest. 'Look very carefully.'

The concierge stiffened, his only gesture a single starched nod.

'Call the manager here.'

'M-M'sieu DuPont? Would you come over?'

The manager obliging with a cordial smile. 'Oui?'

Serault, amiably dubious: 'I was asking about deposit

boxes, how safe yours are . . . I mean, these stories about duplicated keys . . .'

'Here there's but one, the manager's personal responsibility.'

'So your concierge assured me . . . It's never out of your sight?'

'It never leaves me.' The manager twiddling fingers against where his waistcoat pocket would be. 'Not while I'm on duty, M'sieu.'

Serault raised his gun into full view. 'Hands where they are.'

An indignant inhaling. 'Whatever is this, you won't get away – '

'Be quiet.' Serault edging along the counter to the flap, lifting and slipping through. The Vattiers following. 'No noise, no alarms, no trouble, and you'll live to know how we get caught.'

A siren wailed, and for an instant Serault chilled from his own words. Fearing the manager's act of being insulted rather than terrified was due to having already signalled the police. But the manicured hands stayed on the impeccable suit, the siren moved away outside, and the lobby remained desolate. The Prince and his Princess were merely leaving for the palace, and the commoners were gawking in all directions except the right one. Serault relaxing, realizing the inscrutable nature of hotel managers dictated they be insufferable no matter what the occasion. Coming up behind them he said:

'Both of you. Take the satchel into the cashier's cage.'

The manager gripped the handle along with the concierge. The cashier's cage was wire-fenced at the counter and on the side facing the office section. Its back was open and its far side the wall of deposit drawers. Ledgers and calculators.

'Put the satchel on the change desk,' Serault said, and it was so placed, cradled like a baby. 'Now your keys.'

The manager struggling fitfully with himself. 'I'd rather die.'

A swift full-nelson. By Marc without warning, nary a

117

scuffle or choke out of the manager, the concierge looking on with sickened eyes. Serault unbuttoned the manager's jacket.

The manager squirming from the familiarity. 'How dare you.'

'Mondieu, are you banal.' Serault plucking a ring of keys out of the breast pocket. 'Take them to the stockroom and tape them.'

Marc marching the manager, the concierge needing no prompting by Henri, across the office section. To the stockroom, a cramped dusty hollow under the grand mezzanine staircase. While Serault and Kalenberg as a team unlocked the drawers and emptied out whatever they contained. Deeds, certificates, wax-sealed envelopes that crinkled when touched, cash in various currencies, gold bars, silver bars, it all went into the satchel. And when the drawers were reshut, Kalenberg took the satchel and Serault went into the stockroom.

The manager and concierge were taped to a portmandieu, wrists and ankles, back to back. The Vattiers winding handkerchiefs into gags as Serault approached, reaching in his back pocket as if for a gun.

'Don't,' the concierge piping. 'Don't, we'll – '

'What?' Serault smiling genially. 'Identify us?'

'We'll remember to forget.'

'You do that.' And Serault swung a loaded sock to sap them both on the back of the head. He was an amateur at this, not having had practical experience on how hard to hit. He wanted only temporary amnesia and nothing serious, but it was a chancy job, and it made him uneasy and a little regretful. While the Vattiers were gagging the inert men, Serault looked them over, relieved to find he hadn't broken skin, and their breathing, while shallow, was even.

Out of the stockroom door and lock it, pocketing the key. Passing through the flap for the last time; meeting Kalenberg with both satchels at the Horsten display. Serault easing in a key from the second set he'd taken, afraid that if it were the wrong one an alarm could be tripped. Ah, but how nicely the tumblers settled and how sweetly the key turned . . .

A sudden swish of the revolving entrance door. The drunk stumbling into the lobby, his nose like the red rubber bulb of a squeeze spray. 'Hey, you guys, I can't find that restaurant.'

Serault gave a hard look, first at the drunk and then at Henri, who understood and swivelled around, snagging the drunk by the arm. Leading him towards the far end of the lobby. 'Sir, exactly what...'

'Tourists,' Kalenberg muttered as if it were something dirty.

Serault left the key in the lock, releasing the rest to dangle from the ring. Sliding the glass door on rollers that made a faint squeak. With controlled haste they began stripping the cases: gems precious and semiprecious; silver rose rings and gold nose rings; filigree brooches, green onyx pendants, snake chokers with eyes of ruby. Collectors' exotica such as 6-inch Russian peasant figures clad in fur with beards of Norwegian sunstone. A pale jade carving of the goddess Kuan Yin, and intricate Persian hubble-bubble mouthpiece; a sapphire pigeon egg laid in a sterling eagle claw. One two three, the display sucked bare of everything but its supportive statuary. How pleasantly the satchels bulged.

Cases reclosed, satchels strapped. A speedy stroll through the lobby, to the magazine counter. Where Henri had assembled the attaché case, suitcase and portable frame. Saying: 'I poured him out of the side exit, into the Avenue. But we've got to hurry. The crowds are breaking up.'

'We've been less than ten minutes,' Serault replied starting down the hall. 'And we can't work *too* fast; the Palace guards must have time to tuck their royalty to bed.' Then he hesitated. 'Wait. Guards. Marc, you're the guard here. Cover the display with the sheets off the news-stand. It may look peculiar, but it'll look closed.'

'Right.' Marc turning around.

Trucking on. Henri into the men's room, Kalenberg with the satchels, and Serault juggling the two cases and the frame continuing to the Empire Room. Crossing the dim cavern, ominous and still. Tall windows lining their right wove brilliance from the revelry outside to dog their tread. By the vacant bandstand and entering the service pantry, whose back wall was the left panel of the fresco.

Hidden from casual view by the partition, Serault began shoving the counter, glass and silver racks away from the wall. Kalenberg unfolded the frame, fitting it together and adjusting it to the doorway. Serault opened the suitcase, took out a hand-sized ball of plastique. He pressed it navel-high to the middle of the tapestry, and was forming it into a cone when the Vattiers arrived with the men's room door slung between them.

'I covered the display,' Marc said. 'There're a few people in the lobby now, but nobody stopped or questioned us.'

'The bellhop's snoring,' Henri added, lowering his end. 'The guard wanted to know if there's a way to smoke while he's gagged.'

'And the quarantine sign?' Serault was on his knees, rigging one of the remote-control detonators. 'Did you string it across?'

'Soon's we took off the door, René.' Marc righted the door, jostling it against the frame. 'Nobody'll dare go into the bathroom until it's fumigated.' It only took a moment's aligning for him to hang the door, the hinges European, with each hinge leaf having just one knuckle and the hinge pin built into the jamb leaf. He then barred the door with a cross-beam pivoting on the frame, and the men were now completely closed off, able to work freely without attracting closer attention.

'Crouch behind the counter,' Serault said, retreating. 'But keep up on the balls of your feet and breathe through your mouth.'

'Aren't you going to drill holes in the wall?' Henri, nervous, was already flinching. 'Don't you have to pack the charge or something?'

'Not plastique,' Serault answered. 'Bernard can explain the physics, but according to him the stuff blows contrary to common sense, especially when cone-shaped. Its force is directed against resistance instead of away from it.' Then,

120

hunkering down, he opened the attaché case and extended its antenna. 'Ready?'

'These damn gizmos better work, is all,' Marc said, fingers in his ears and eyes squeezed closed. 'We've worked too hard.'

'Well, if they don't, we've got two fine satchels as consolation.' Serault felt exquisite. The first segment had unfolded perfectly and there was no drawing back. Just garlands and winged griffons between them and Cartier. 'Ah!' he said and pressed the buttons.

The buttons sending the tone calls,
the tone calls keying the squelches,
the squelches closing the relays,
the relays tripping the mouse traps,
the mouse traps driving the nail heads,
('cept for ones yanking the flare caps),
the nail heads striking the primers . . .
now hear the Word of the Lord.

Chapter Fifteen

An instant of stillness as if of failure. Then:

The top of Mont-Agel grew an extra few metres, the television relay one of the smaller chunks hurtling. Tree limbs and shards of leaves splayed from the eruption, stone and wood rained back into the newly formed crater. TV-Monte-Carlo had been off the air anyway, its normal programming ending at 10:50 after the prime-time movie *Three Smart Girls* with Deanna Durbin. It would not be beaming again that night, emergency or no. Nearer Mont-Gros, the radio tower was tilting, one leg crumpled, the rock beneath fragmented. Earth and shredded pine cascaded with the cable down a steep slope, carrying the Voice of Monaco, who never ceased till two, over the brink while spinning St Elmo's Fire hot new disc *Moody Orifice* for Ricky and Dicky and Nicky and Biffy and all of you garçons et filles at Rosey's. Over the brink into the blissful calm of the abyss below . . .

A belch like a cannon blew Claude Raynal awake. He thrashed in his blanket, hearing his wife in the next room. 'Jenny? Jenny!'

'Claude, oh là là!'

Struggling from the bedroom into the glaring kitchen. Where his wife who'd been baking was at the window, staring out intently.

'What is it, Jenny? What's wrong?'

'The radio went dead. Pouf like that.'

'For that you won't let me sleep?'

'And where the post office was is now a big hole.'

Raynal went to look alongside his wife, nose pressed to the glass and groggily squinting. On comfortable residential Rue de la Colle, he could see lights and figures huddled at windows as he was. Directly across the street, the substation had cracks like tree roots growing all up its walls, its tile roof no longer in existence. And a curl of grey smoke was wafting volcanic from the interior. Above and about, white ash fluttered downward to sprinkle the debris cluttering the sidewalk. Raynal watched the flakes, shaking his head.

'Snow? In August, Jenny, in Monaco?'

'Claude, wake up. It's not snowing. Those are letters.'

'Foutoir!' Raynal cursed, turning away to bustle into the living room, impassioned to report this outrage against public decency. But when he telephoned the police, nobody answered . . .

Agent Guillaume of the Sûreté Publique was lounging in the communications room, reading a paperback thriller that had been taken from a prisoner and was making the rounds of headquarters. Nothing better to do during his shift; the gala was SBM's headache, and the random murmurs coming from his transceiver were few and dull. He was on the page where the Cairo belly-dancer twirled her tassels in opposing directions to better double-cross the hero, and was sadly ruminating the fact that should his wife try such a feat she'd be dusting the floors, when the basement garage blew apart.

A blast deep and terrible rising up. Guillaume feeling the shock wave pass through the floor and jiggle his chair. Another – the noise more snappish, yet at the same time muffled and confined. He sprang for the door without fully thinking why, out into the turmoil of agents and secretaries milling in the hall. All talking at once.

'What's happened? What's happened?'

'Revolution!'

'The trumpet has blown and we're on the wrong shore!'

'A van exploded in the garage,' a girl said, intercom in hand.

'The petrol tanks, the grease! Guillaume, call the firemen!'

Guillaume ducked into the communications room just as another agent suggested calling the police. But Guillaume could not call anybody, for strangely the transceiver was now dead. In a fretful manner, tubes humming with eagerness, yet no response, no pulse, no readings on the meters. Worse, the room was filling with orange-red smoke that writhed from the air vents like psychedelic pop art. Guillaume, coughing and choking, backed out into the hall where the haze hung less thick. Close by in the commandant's office, barking could be heard, terminated by a grand crash. Before Guillaume or the other agents could reach the office door, it was punctured by a bellowed order:

'Grand Dieux! Abandon ship! All hands abandon ship!'

The headquarters was evacuated with informal promptness. A lively disregard for procedures and etiquette, ladies first if they elbowed their way there, the men bounding the stairs and packing the lift, wedging and cursing their way to safety. The commandant, having tripped over Yvonne and cracked his ankle, had to be carted outside in a wheelbarrow, his dog riding on his stomach.

. . . And up on Avenue des Beaux-Arts, two SBM guards were patrolling. Not expecting any trouble, the Family having left and the crowds beginning to thin. Their tour would be a lark from here on in.

A shattering roar rattled their complacency.

Alphonse took a step back. On Gaston's shoe, Gaston groaning and shoving him off. 'The Hôtel, I think it came from there.' Not waiting for his partner, Gaston limped around the corner by Cartier and glanced into the Empire Room. It was dark and quiet, undisturbed.

Alphonse was now waving madly. 'Up the street. Up the street.'

At a rapid pace to the end of Beaux-Arts. To stare disbelievingly at the substation. It was boiling over with reddish densely acrid fumes, and from around the side where the basement was came the fragile crackling of a fire. The three agents on duty were out on the sidewalk, gulping and wheezing to clear their lungs.

Gaston gestured towards them. 'We've got to help!'

'The Casino . . .' Both guards eyed each other with rising concern. 'Alphonse, do you suppose something more serious . . . ?'

'We'd best check.' A final glimpse of the substation. Then, with duty beckoning, they hustled back towards the Place . . .

In the police basements, the two ruptured vans had immediately tripped automatic heat sensors. Already trucks and men were racing from the fire stations, converging on the narrow strip of La Condamine and Avenue Princess Alice. Bewildered policemen tried spasmodically to keep some form of order, while firemen charged the buildings brandishing axes and hoses as if to do battle. The sudden flood of fire equipment clogging the streets, blocking traffic wanting to pass and attracting spectators liking fires. Generating still more confusion and general snarl . . .

Ledoux heard the explosions, threw his brush into a can, ripped off the last of the masking tape, and swung wide the garage doors. Trusting the wind to dry his fresh paint. Careening down the alleyway, switching on his flasher and siren, seeing shifting distant tongues of smoke laving skyward as if from funeral pyres. Nearing the centre of town, clouds growing, other sirens now mingling with his own. Thrusting down Allée des Boulingrins, praying by Patron Saint Subdolous he wouldn't mash a stray pedestrian, straight along the terrace hedge to whip in by the front of the Hôtel.

Quickly to the back of the ambulance, his white smock outlined by the revolving blue light. Up with the lid and out with the fancy stretcher which Kalenberg had delivered just that afternoon, complete with chrome railing sides and fat rubber tyres and a coverlet concealing the deflated poupée doll. The fires reflecting hideously in window panes and the faces of people. Smoke overlay the Place like gauze, making a coppery halo silhouetting the Hôtel. There was erratic shouting and milling, some fearful, some excited, some too drunk to know what the hell. Ledoux watched it all for a moment, then lowered his head and massaged his face.

It was like a Second Coming. A Second Coming that could be his second chance.

Chapter Sixteen

The fresco leapt out at them.

A funnel of concrete and tapestry spewing against the counter, the blast punching a jagged circle through the wall. Minor in comparison to the other simultaneous explosions, but stunning, popping eardrums in the confined pantry. Dust and mortar settling in the momentary vacuum, silting the numbed men.

Serault straightened, brushing himself off. Stepped to the hole, and, with a small prybar, widened the gap enough to crawl through. Into the black hole of Cartier. Henri passed the suitcase to him and followed, the only other one sufficiently slim. Kalenberg and Marc stayed in the pantry according to plan and constitution.

The shop, small and elite, had steel blinds lowered over its windows and door to protect it against burglars. For which Serault was thankful, shining a pencil flash around the darkness. Waves of grit and the stench of explosive washed over his face. A hillock of rubble flowed on the plush carpet, incongruous to the dignified décor of embossed wallpaper and mahogany wainscotting. A series of cabinets ran in front and to their right; a leather-topped desk and a safe the size of a closet were on their left. The safe was wedged flush against the back corner, the type with scrolling on the sides and large castors underneath, as if nothing short of an elephant herd could budge it.

Serault took the suitcase to the safe, saying: 'Check outside,' pressing another, smaller ball of plastique like chewing gum between the dial and the lever. He stuck a time-fuse pencil into the wad, took two pillowslips out of the suitcase and shut it, and turned to Henri, who was peering through the slats of one window. 'Well?'

'Nothing,' Henri whispered. 'Nobody special out – Wait!' He dropped to his knees. 'Two SBM guards. They're heading this way.'

Serault forced himself to remain absolutely still, hearing the shoes running down Beaux-Arts. Henri's fright fed and perched upon his own. Judas priest, it's not that I'm precisely panicked yet, but I am becoming overwhelmed. In which case I might suddenly shout HELP GET ME OUT OF THIS and then what? Only psychopaths can afford much less withstand such suspense ...

The footsteps passed and magically kept moving.

Henri slowly inched up again to see through the shutters. 'Eh. They're crossing the Place now, going to the café.'

Serault released a sigh: I've got to cultivate a better sense of resignation. In this world or out of it, most of the time most of us make our own luck ... He snapped the pencil at its shortest mark, vaulting the room to huddle with Henri behind a cabinet.

'Six sec –'

A spank of light, a kick of thunder.

'Impatient devils.' Serault up and to the smouldering safe, fitting the sharpened prong of the prybar under the combination dial. The dial fell off with the ease of a coat button, its shaft still attached. Serault reached in the shaft's hole and turned the broken catch with his fingers. Then shoved the lever downward, the haemorrhaged gears scraping, inner bolts grinding, the door yawning open ...

And in the police headquarters and substations, lights flickered on the monitoring panels. To flash with others glowing since they'd been triggered by alarms built into Cartier's walls. Lonely lamps. Nobody at the communications desks to notice them. The buildings abdicated to a cotton smog, some of it greasy brown but mostly that weird cloying rouge that stifled the lungs ...

Serault held the pencil flash by his teeth, smiling with his lips bared back. At bald beady stones, and precision settings, and luxurious trinkets stamped with the three interlinking rings, the hallmark of Cartier. Sliding from velvet trays into the pillowslip as fast as he could tip. Perspiration spotting his forehead, breath harsh in the stifling pungency of the room. Aware that behind him Henri was busily at work, tidying up the cabinets.

To the hole, handing through a full sack. Marc there to receive, his face appearing to announce: 'Bernard's here with the doll.'

'Good. Hurry with her, we've just a bit left and we're done.'

Marc nodding, withdrawing. Placing the sack next to the satchels and fishing out his pocket knife. As Kalenberg uncovered the poupée. And Ledoux rested against the partition, sighing: 'I thought I'd perish from worry or sinus or both or neither before I could – Sacre!'

'Eh?' Marc jerking, almost cutting his thumb. 'The cops?'

'For a second there, I'd have sworn she was real.'

Marc giving Ledoux a nasty look, then giving the doll an examination. For like Ledoux, this was the first time he'd seen her unpacked. Unrolled and stretched flat on the stretcher, naked with honey-blonde hair, a vapid pout, and a seamless, flesh-tinted body of idealistically proportioned plastic. Inflated she might have passed for a stewardess. Marc rolled her on her stomach, puncturing her coccyx. 'Eh, and she's already half full of machinery,' he said, slitting her up the spine.

Kalenberg opened a satchel, bristling. 'I searched hard to find the most lifelike,' he said, pouring jewellery inside her cavity. 'Could I help she came with accessories?'

'You did well.' Ledoux agitated her feet, settling the contents down her hollow legs. 'Don't mind me. My mental state isn't the firmest or finest, not that I claimed it ever was.'

Marc picked up the pillowslip and was beginning to shake it when there came a rattling of the door. He clamped a hand over the mouth of the slip, everyone poised rigid. More rattling. Then a blurred voice: 'Is this one occupied? Hey in there, have a heart.'

'Mein Gott,' Kalenberg whispered. 'That drunk again.'

A thumping on the door. 'Hey fellah, don't sit there all night.'

'Drunk?' Ledoux perplexed, but nobody answering. Kalenberg wheeled the stretcher aside, Marc thrust the sack at Ledoux and opened the door just wide enough for the man to see his uniform. He said in English: 'This toilette is temporarily out of communion.'

'Yeah, but officer, the other one has a disease.'

'We're investigating.' Marc locked the door again.

A renewed spasm of activity. The pillowslip upended and the second satchel emptied, the doll taking her lumps, no time to waste organizing her innards, the drunk still mumbling on the other side of the partition. Serault crawled through, pushing the suitcase ahead of him, Henri at his heels with the second pillowslip. Marc put a finger to his lips in an old-fashioned sign for silence, and Serault and Henri, now hearing the drunk, understood.

The pantry was a tight squeeze what with five men and the stretcher. A little agile dancing, though, and the doll was filled, slips tucked around the loot, and her plastic sides pressed in so Ledoux could close her wound with alligator clips. She was revolved, looking somewhat like a Rubens nude with mumps. Marc kneaded and massaged her into a more natural shape, for the thirty seconds Henri took wadding his coat into the suitcase and slipping the tails from his trousers, smoothing the wrinkles out of his tuxedo jacket.

'Set?' Serault asked softly, glancing for anything missed. Everybody nodded, glancing about with him.

'Any questions about the next part – or if we should try it?' Everybody shook their heads.

The door jerked open and Ledoux, the first one out, rolled the stretcher imperiously. 'Oyez! Make way!' Serault with his attaché case, Henri with the satchels, Kalenberg tagging with the suitcase and Marc trailing as rear guard. The drunk, startled, agape.

130

'I've got the DTs! All you plus a dame in there?'

'That's what we're investigating,' Marc replied sagely.

Serault circled around and rapped the man with his weighted sock. They carried him into the pantry, left him lying on the counter with his arms folded, and ran out, slamming the door so hard the cross-bar dropped of its own volition across the frame.

Trundling back the way they'd come. Out of the Empire Room and down the hallway. The men's room an unlit tomb, a black rope stretched across the bare doorway, a red-bordered notice dangling from it, warning of infection. Past a set of advertising posters – drink scotch, smoke filters, ride trains. Serault's crack streamliner, Route of the Scalded Cat. Crossing the lobby without pausing for whistle-stops or milk-runs or the helpless milling throng.

'Oyez! Oyez!'

Through the swing-door beside the revolving entrance. Negotiating the steps, Ledoux holding one end of the stretcher, Kalenberg the bereaved husband lugging the other. Serault trotting ahead as a good manager should, to open the ambulance's tail gate. Henri tossed in the satchels, slid in Kalenberg's suitcase and helped lift the stretcher inside. Marc, as all policemen do, kept the curious at bay; make room make room give the lady air please.

'See you in a few hours,' Serault said to Ledoux. Ledoux smiled weakly as he started the motor. He watched the four rush up the steps and back into the Hôtel; no gunshots or yells, those hours may pass safely yet. He started around the Place at a brisk tempo. Past the casino brightly lit, a senile dowager impervious to reality. By an SBM guard a foot from his open window, Ledoux tensing but grimly persevering. Alongside the Magpie Café, to the corner –

A shrill police whistle. Glancing in his mirror, Ledoux saw the guard sprinting, motioning him to halt. Ledoux pulling over to the kerb with puckered sphyncter muscles, able to outrun the man but not his radio. Trapped – yet how to escape when he himself is the trap?

The guard called out: 'M'sieu, your plate is dragging.'

131

Ledoux patted his cheeks. 'Mais non. My teeth are in fine – '

'Your licence plate.' The guard pointed to the rear bumper.

Ledoux got out and walked back. 'Why, you're right, it is. A bolt must've worked loose. I'll fix it as soon as I get to the clinic.'

'I'm sorry, but the law is you can't proceed on dangling plates.'

'But my patient! It's an emergency!'

Stubbornly: 'The law has no exceptions. The law clearly states – '

'I know, I know.' Ledoux scanned the street and checked his pockets frantically for something to hold up the plate. Finding nothing but the empty package for the clips. Clips? With mounting despair, he opened the tail gate and reached in under the stretcher's coverlet. Sensing the guard's surprised eyes on his intimate fumblings. 'It's not what it seems,' he said over his shoulder. 'Believe me.'

The guard leaning in. 'My, a young lady. What happened?'

'A wee accident at the Hôtel.'

'Ah!' The guard triumphant. 'So there *was* an explosion in there.'

'No explosion, sir.' Ledoux a montage of chagrin and innocence. 'Lady Bercail had her panties hooked by a trout fly and fell into a fit. Hates being touched.' The blanket shifting, exposing more of the doll the more Ledoux tried groping for her clips. 'The maid was responsible, urging the earl to flex his pole. There, got one.'

Ledoux brought out the clip. The guard leaned in further, clucking his tongue in lecherous sympathy. 'Poor girl, she'll catch a cold,' wrapping the blanket solicitously around her, tucking it up under her arms. Where in the left pit came a click like a switch strategically placed. From her loins began an inexplicable strum, her hips started to rotate and her thighs to undulate upwards.

'By the harem of God!' The guard sprang back in shock.

'Why . . .' Ledoux, caught just as unaware, inwardly

132

cursed Kalenberg and his pet project. 'Why . . . look what you've done, sir.'

'Me? I haven't done anything! And what're all those noises?'

'You touched her. She's thrown another fit, suffering as she does from an on and off form of trachilics.' The poupée continued her grinding technique, the batterized motor in her buttocks humming as if moaning, the jewellery continuously clashing and scraping together. 'Technically known as staff and distaff, or if you prefer the Latin, quid est pablum in a three-phrase conjugation.'

The guard horrified. 'Get her out of here! Forget your damn plate, and forget I ever touched her! I'll deny everything under oath!'

'At once, sir.' Ledoux closing the lid on her clatter, clambering back behind the wheel. 'And sir, I've forgotten already.'

The guard stared at the ambulance departing. Standing wilted, blotting his forehead with the back of his sleeve.

His partner crossed the street from the café, chewing a Mars bar. 'Boisterous in there but not out of control. What were you doing?'

'Nothing. Never mind. It was an ambulance, is all.'

'Odd coloured ambulance, Gaston, painted brown that way.'

'I'm in no mood for humour, Alphonse. It was white as chalk.'

Alphonse lowered his Mars bar. 'Are you feeling ill? I was standing right over there on the kerb and I know brown when I see it.'

'Impossible. It's not one of the primary colours.'

'If you're casting aspersions to my intelligence, I wouldn't if I were you. Not a man who signs his name with an X. Furthermore – '

Attention! Attention!

Both men snapped up their walkie-talkies, putting the tinny sound to their ears. From the casino the SBM dispatcher broadcast: *All patrols, remain in your positions for*

133

new orders. Repeat: all patrols, remain in your position for new orders.

Gaston reclipped his walkie-talkie, glancing above the Hôtel where smoke coiled like stationary feathers. Then a breeze lightly stirred, jumbling light and shadow, only to die and let the plumes re-form. He said thoughtfully, 'Something's awfully wrong tonight.'

'Yes, I feel it now all of a sudden. To do with those fires.'

'Alphonse, I don't see how. They're none of our affair . . .'

. . . Ledoux tearing out of the Place and up Avenue de Madone. Hounded by nightmares of police pursuit, a flight brief and futile, the death of a loved one. Namely himself. Pawing the passenger seat for the two canisters of tyre-bursters left there on purpose, in case of emergencies like this. Prying their tops off with his teeth and flinging handfuls of the sharp-pronged spikes out of the window, then throwing the empty tins out after them when he came to the Boulevard des Moulins, the main route east from Monte Carlo. Turning the corner without clearing right of way, he barely, but barely, missed smearing car and self against the side of a refrigerated meat truck.

At Monaco's boundary he veered up a side street. Crossing the Moyenne Corniche and continuing along a corkscrew short cut to Roquebrune. Considerable dodging of potholes and parked cars, Ledoux relying on accelerator and steering, siren and flasher off to make things harder to trace. Swerving onto the thin lane leading up to the village itself, coasting to a stop in front of Serault's door, not pausing for breath but rolling the stretcher at once into the house. Then he removed satchels, suitcase, rack, siren, flasher and other portable accessories from the wagon, for they were to be buried as well. Carting back and forth with cautious grace, though doubting he'd encounter any of the natives. Like everybody else who's Nobody, they'd all be asleep at this hour.

Front door bolted. Toting everything to the cellar, saving the cumbersome poupée for the last. Stumbling on the last steps of the spiral staircase, almost sprawling when he dropped her to the floor. Near him, where it was mostly

134

rock and original castle foundation, sacks of ready-mix concrete were piled along with tarpaulin, shovels, tampers, and a hose squirrelling down from the kitchen sink.

Ledoux threw his equipment into the hole. The doll he dragged over as he might a corpse, lining it up with the side of the hole and rolling her in, where she dropped flat as if in a grave. She'd long since stopped twitching, the batteries having run down, and she just lay there staring up with her blank pathetic smile. Giving Ledoux the creeps.

He covered her with his intern's smock and went upstairs in search of a drink. There was more to do – he had to sneak the car back to Monaco, scrub it and the garage and return to help with the floor – but that could wait. More important was a dram of cognac, to dispel the chill from the *cave* and enervate the soul. Slowly the calipers constricting his heart began to loosen, and he began wondering how the others were faring at the gala. His worry an abstraction for him, since he was effectively out of the operation, and yet a wondering, a hoping all the same that it would all work.

Chapter Seventeen

The guard sitting in the casino cloakroom asked: 'What's going on out there?'

'A fire, I think.' Serault shrugged. 'I could be mistaken.'

'Well, whatever it is, it's upset the gala.' The guard atwitch, rubbing his elbow. 'Some guests have actually been thinking of leaving early, before the fireworks display. Disgraceful.'

'If I were you I'd advise them to stay.' Serault smiled with reassurance. 'At least until things are clear, more normal. Not that it's anything serious, you understand; already the sirens have stopped. Merely an accident picking a bad night to happen.'

'Maybe. Maybe so . . .'

The guard rubbing and sighing. Watching the quartet who'd just come up in the passageway lift walk past his desk and turn left, entering the main hall. A Somebody from the Hôtel with his own guard, and two purposeful gentlemen with their tickets in order. The least of his worries. Far more distressing were these silly patrons pestering with questions, and those bizarre rumours floating from the outside world . . . The guard glanced from his desk to the cloakroom attendant, a frail woman who was resting arms and breasts on the counter, listening. Ears like brass trumpets, she had. He voiced an errant, nervous thought to her: 'Though I've never been much for believing in coincidence . . .'

Images passed in the mirrors lining the hallway. Serault leaning forward, smoothly intense as if on castors. Kalenberg with a plump expression behind his glasses. Henri stern yet

136

gangly in Ledoux's tuxedo, belying the chestnut that clothes make the man. Marc loping in his pigeon-toed gait, head tilted slightly as if hearing faint music: perhaps that of the violins straining up behind them from the terrace, stridently recapturing attentions sent wandering by fires and explosions. Most of the guests remaining down there with the orchestra, though a growing number were clustering in the halls. Clotting noisily, wavering and indecisive.

The four men rounded the ell, crossing the northern half of the entrance hall. Main doors on their left. Serault gesturing with his attaché case to an obscure door beside them. 'The basement.'

Kalenberg and Henri branching towards it without reply.

Serault and Marc moving straight, not breaking stride. Nearing the discreet corridor which led to the security office. A guard was standing there, looking more wary, more edgy and cynical than the older guard stationed in the cloakroom.

'René,' Marc whispered. 'René, he's not supposed to be there.'

Serault unperturbed, feeling confident. It'd taken less than ten minutes for the Hôtel and a bit over that for Cartier; they were ahead of schedule and the next fifteen, twenty minutes promised long-awaited gratification. He could afford a certain magnanimity of spirit. 'Advantage out of disadvantage, Marc, that's the secret.'

'I'll savour your maxim on a rainy afternoon. What about now?'

'Ah well . . . Our drunk routine proved a hit once before.'

Approaching. The guard tensing, blocking their path. Serault set his case down. Marc made as if to brush past, the guard turned towards Marc and raised his arm. 'Your authorization, s'il vous plait.'

'That's what we're investigating,' Marc said.

The guard stuck out his tongue and fell into Marc's arms. 'Look, he needs help.' Serault pocketed his sock, taking his case and starting down the corridor. 'We now have an excuse and a distraction, Marc. Two definite advantages, eh?'

Marc backed after Serault, the guard clasped under his

arms in a lifesaver's hug. Head lolling, arms dragging, knuckles grazing the tile floor. Marc rubbed shoulders with the corridor wall, struggling to the end where there was a door that had a brass plate: SÛRETÉ and a one-way glass window. Pausing while Serault pushed insistently on the button beside it.

From the grille above the button: 'Yes?'

Serault in an urgent tremolo: 'Your guard, he has fainted.'

'Is he sick?'

'Am I a doctor? Fainted I tell you, and very suddenly at that.'

'Take him to the infirmary.'

The tiny loudspeaker on the grille reduced any tone to flat indifference. Serault on the other hand intensifying his arousal with gestures and pitch of voice. '*You* take him. He's *your* guard.'

'. . . Just a moment, sir.'

There was one of those hesitations denoting indecision, filled with a conference Serault could not see nor hear but only assume. Marc leaned against the door, trying to appear exhausted and disgusted from his exertion. Furtively eyeing Serault. Serault about to press the button and his argument again, when the latch buzzed. Marc elbowed the door, feeling the lock click and give.

A procession. Serault first, shifting aside for Marc, the door closing automatically on the guard's dragging heels. The office square, dour, table and chairs to the right, wall map and filing cabinets on the left, communications desk directly ahead. The desk was a semicircular console of meters switches and buttons; microphone coiling outwards on a gooseneck; a loudspeaker lisping static on top. Beside, a bank of three closed-circuit televisions monitored the rake of croupiers, the swirl of dancers, the boiled shirts and breasts that had congealed into bosoms, their small silent screens reducing the casino's interior and terrace to shades of grey. Condensing the gala into some other, different illusion, more on the scale of a stilted von Stroheim artifice.

There were two guards in the office. One acting as the

dispatcher, sitting at the console, half-swivelled around from curiosity. He looked like a bird, a young terrier-faced bird with uniform plumage and bushy hair like black feathers from under the crest of his cap. The other guard was much older, had bat ears and blank watery eyes and just stood there as if waiting to be wound up. Next to him, a pink pudding of a man with a fringe of white hair, and pudgy fingers that kept worrying the buttons of a dark suit just like Serault's.

'Come on, give a hand.' Serault glided behind the older guard, placed his case beside the dispatcher and averted his face to slip on a rubber costume head he'd taken from his pocket. This single polished manoeuvre coincided with the awkward guard reaching. And Marc managing to drop his unconscious guard an instant before the other could help. The other grunting, bending over –

Marc kneed him on the chin. A sharp crunch, and the guard settled flaccid across the first, while Marc drew his automatic and pivoted towards the two remaining men. 'Freeze,' he said.

They did. Riveted with accumulated shock, the marvel of one inert guard compounded by another dropping, then pyramiding as this third guard pointed a gun at them. It was too much to digest.

And then there was this gorilla.

Where the nice executive had been, and wearing his suit and gloves. Covering the dispatcher with yet another gun. His voice muffled and glottal, befitting his appearance: 'Disarm – quick!'

The dispatcher twitched his shoulders, eyes narrowing, but carefully unholstered his service revolver. Serault thought: he's my caution, the only one I've got to keep free and he's feisty. Why couldn't the dispatcher have been the fat man . . . ? Who was darting distraught glances about, patting his pockets as if searching for a stray ticket. A career and a pension to consider and his sick leave was all used up; he was not interested in arguing. Grinning sickly, fumbling a flat Astra .25 from his inner folds.

139

Marc meanwhile was gagging and taping together the guards on the floor. Collecting the guns next, then telling the fat man to kneel, tying his hands behind him, while Serault told the dispatcher:

'You. Radio your men outside to stay where they are.'

The dispatcher was staring at the fat man. 'I can't do that.' Staring as the fat man bleakly rolled over and allowed Marc to wrap his ankles and wad a handkerchief in his mouth. Serault motioned for Marc to exchange places with him, going over to the fat man and hunkering. Placing the muzzle of his gun against his ear and looking up at the dispatcher. 'How many children will he be leaving?'

The fat man jellied, an oblique and begging roll to his eyes. The dispatcher rubbed his knees, swallowing thickly . . . nodded and switched on the mike. 'Attention, all external patrols . . . Remain in position until further orders.'

'And your inside men are to herd the guests to La Salle Garnier.'

Itchy fingers tweaked at controls. 'Attention, internal units and housemen. Advise and assemble all patrons – '

' – and all personnel including the orchestra.'

Again the dispatcher hesitated, appalled.

'*Everybody*,' Serault insisted. 'Leave everything as it is, go in the theatre and shut the doors. It's for their own health.'

The dispatcher blinking and scowling, but his choice was simple. Virtually Aristotelian. The safety of the guests was primary, and gathered in the Salle Garnier at least there'd be plenty of staff to protect them. Moreover, the safety of himself and his worming superior depended on it. Rigid, face waxen, he broadcast. Pushing the mike aside when done, hunching and brooding.

On the monitors, heavyset men were sidling with a whisper here and a gesture there. Gaming tables closing one by one as if wired on some electrical string. Half-empty glasses and unfolded napkins littered the terrace, the bandstand abandoned, streamers and fishnet loitering in the soft breeze. Guests shuffling in perplexed clots of twos and threes, a few singles straggling to join more garrulous friends . . .

A red lamp winked on the console.

'Van Cleef's?' Serault asked.

'It's being broken – ' The dispatcher realizing now, his dawning face growing pink and shiny. 'Saloud,' he said to himself.

Serault said, 'Switch a set to show La Salle Garnier.'

'Saloud,' the dispatcher mumbled again under his breath, his initial surprise on the wane and being replaced by growing resentment. Reluctantly changing channels on the right-hand monitor, tuning in the preposterous baroque theatre. Where people were swelling aisles and filling seats, more jamming through the rear doors and forcing those ahead to swarm towards the stage. On which a frenetic and somewhat stunned André Rasseaux was trying to retune his orchestra.

Ah well, Serault thought, this skirmish is almost won. It is also the weakest link in our elaborate chain of events, when the group is split and vulnerable if anything backfires. But I've handled the risks as adequately if not better than could be expected, and the night will have to be played as it's dealt. Fundamentally, I've no more choice than the dispatcher, considering the alternatives and my basic disposition . . .

Yet despite his efforts to be resigned, Serault had a sensation of uneasiness. Fearful of relying on the same combination of luck and improvisation which had wiped him out so many times here while gambling. He could feel the thin edge of his confidence begin to unravel as the minutes gradually seeped by . . .

On the left-hand screen two tuxedoes appeared in the Salons Privés, their images dim as they flitted across the shadowed field of the camera. The dispatcher made a small jerking lurch, choking out, 'No. You can't do this, not in the casino.'

'Calm, calm. It's one of those things.'

'You're in there.' The dispatcher's meaning askew but he was uncaring. 'Just like Van Cleef's, you're down in there too.'

'Be reasonable.'

141

'In THE casino!' The dispatcher's expression of frustration and indignation merged into a contortion of mania. Calm and reason had boxed him into this; only insane rage could salvage what was left of his pride, his duty. He came up out of the chair, flailing with unexpected venom. Marc moved quickly, quicker, blocking the explosion of flesh with the palm of one hand, a mitt for the dispatcher's face. The dispatcher squirrelling, lurching hard against the console, dropping back into his seat. Hand pressed to his nose, blood welling between his clenched fingers.

'Oh,' his voice nasal, 'what'd you have to do that for?'

'The second time,' Marc said, tight within his own anger.

'My nose is bleeding.'

'It's not my fault.' Marc offered the last of his handkerchiefs. 'Second time tonight somebody's tried to jump me.'

Another red lamp was pulsating on the console.

Serault came over. 'That light, what's it mean?'

The dispatcher studied it. 'It means you should give up.'

A cold delicate quiver moved through Serault. 'What!'

'Yes, surrender. I must've bumped the button in our scuffle, an accident but the damage is done. We've alerted every Gendarmerie and police station from Nice to Menton. M'sieu, the general alarm.'

'Well, stop it! Call them off!'

The dispatcher bunched Marc's handkerchief against his nose, and, in spite of his chagrin and pain, began to smile. A treacly smile with overtones of malice. He said: 'I cannot.'

Chapter Eighteen

Kalenberg descended, Henri close behind. On time-scalloped stairs that curled in a lazy spiral, reaching the basement where corridors branched like dark-panelled spokes. Henri with his hand in his jacket, drawing his automatic. 'Not here,' Kalenberg gripping an arm. 'Not now.'

'But if somebody comes . . .'

'Then we're merely curious guests and very sorry.' Kalenberg began stalking to the right, ponderous on musty floral carpet, passing thick recessed doorways and brass pendant lamps. Henri plucked at his sleeve. Kalenberg turning. 'Ja?'

'These doors all look alike. We could pick the wrong one.'

'Impossible.'

'But we've never been down here before. How can you tell?'

'Mathematical deduction. I paced from Van Cleef's entrance to the outside corner of the casino, and then to the main doors. In the lobby I paced to the basement door, subtracted and allowed for suitable adjustments in building thickness. Now I'm retracing.'

Henri seemed unconvinced. 'We could get lost even.'

Kalenberg peevishly tapped his temple. 'Trust me.'

Creeping onwards, turning left now into another corridor, Kalenberg moved in fits and tangoes, slowing to estimate his distances, then quick-quick only to slow again, each time shaking his head. Distracting Henri who was peering in all directions at once. Coming finally to a door like all the others, where Kalenberg stopped.

143

'Van Cleef's, Henri.' Bending to put his eye to the keyhole. 'My computations are perfect and exact. This is it, I know it.' Gently turning the handle. 'It's too dark to see anything inside, Henri, so get your torch ready. Strange, the door is unlocked – '

Kalenberg stiffened, abruptly silent.

Sounds of querulous voices came drifting towards them.

Kalenberg wrenched the door open, Henri on his back and slamming the door after them. An undignified plunge into utter blackness, solid and frightening, Kalenberg landing against the spaghetti of a damp mophead, the wedge of his foot in a bucket he couldn't see.

Tottering, choking a reflexive wail, fumbling for his balance. Something hit him in the paunch and he nearly sat down.

'Grab me there again,' Henri said, 'and I'll really wreck you.'

'Quiet.' Kalenberg leaned on the mop, using it as a crutch.

Footsteps and muted words came closer, stopping in front of the cleaners' cupboard. Kalenberg stood motionless, teeth clenched until he could feel his fillings. Henri breathed shallowly, slighty crouching. Waiting . . . More conversation, more waiting . . . The wait suddenly ending when somewhere a door closed and there was silence. Another minute to make sure, then Henri peeked outside.

The corridor was empty.

'Trust me,' he mimicked, stepping out.

'It must be the next one then.' Kalenberg disentangled himself from the mop and bucket. 'Just be thankful for a closet when it was needed. Besides, you're the one who has the torch.'

The next door was locked.

Henri asked: 'Prybar?'

'Too sturdy.' Kalenberg pinched a corner off the thin slab of plastique he was carrying in his breast pocket, moulding the nubbin into the keyhole. Took a time-fuse from the same pocket, tucked it in the hole like a thermometer . . . and hesitated.

144

Henri, impatiently: 'Now what?'

'Too noisy.' To the closet, keeping the door ajar to see by, returning with an economy-sized box of detergent powder, which he pressed against the latch after first snapping off the pencil.

A muffled, discreet burp came from the door. The woodwork bulged slightly, relaxing, smoking. Kalenberg tenderly removed the box which had grown a hole in its front, handing the box to Henri and swinging the door open. Catching the remains of the lock, pins like rotten teeth falling from the shattered ward.

Henri followed Kalenberg inside. He set down the leaky box to bring out a flat pocket torch. 'I bet the alarm's gone off upstairs,' he murmured, closing the door and seeing a relay switch dangling from the jamb. 'Hope my brother and René are all right.'

'Over here with the light.' Kalenberg studied another, inner door of steel bars: with the exit closed, the effect was that of a prison cell. Henri illuminated, and Kalenberg blasted the second door. To step through, into the Van Cleef showroom. Chic with cream, the left wall impressive with its vault, door circular and complex like the hatch of a submarine.

They headed straight for the vault, around a corner and over a railing. Hidden from the street by the same type of metal window blinds which had shuttered Cartier's windows. Henri held the light steady, leaning over Kalenberg. 'Any problems?'

Kalenberg inspected, philosophically shrugging. 'Who's to say? This is old explosive; I am a new expert.' Rolling the plastique strip into a ball and slapping it against the door. 'Too much and we earn the men across the hall. Too little and we don't earn the jewels.' Breaking another time fuse. They leaped together over the railing, sinking into the carpet. 'One, two, three, four, five – '

They swayed in the sudden heat, the eruption of crimson and white like the bursting of a rotten egg. Then to the blackened door through an eddy of plaster and ornament,

145

Kicking away the debris. Fearing the charge hadn't been powerful enough. Tugging, twisting madly at the large round wheel, hysteria mounting almost to the point of turning and running. Then the door made a dismal grating sound and fell off, rotating to the floor.

Thrusting over it, into the vault. 'The sacks, Henri, the sacks.' Kalenberg unbuttoned his shirt, removing one of the pillowslips he'd been wearing underneath. Henri did the same, one-handed, the other still holding the torch. Whose beams were touching a crystalline world, the vault lined with tiers filled with stones and settings. Refractions of facet and fire. As from left to right, top to bottom, trays were upended into the sacks.

'Wesley's passion was Van Cleef's.' Kalenberg staggered weighted from the vault. 'He should be here, he truly should.'

'And we should not.' Henri moved for the railing and door of steel bars. Kalenberg caught him before he could exit into the hall. 'Wait, listen first . . .'

Pausing, Henri traded his gun for the torch. Hearing nothing. Darting out then and down the hall, automatic levelled and sack over his left shoulder. Kalenberg scuttled after, reflecting how impetuous Henri was and questioning how effective a single gun, or even two including his own, would be against hardened professionals. Thinking how, if it came to trouble, his best chance lay in abandoning the bag and making a berserk gallop. Never mind where.

The corridors stretched endless, the stairs seemed shifted to some distant country. Finally arriving, climbing the steps half-expecting hordes to be clustering above for the capture. Gently Henri pushed open the door. The lobby was a mausoleum.

Shuttling sacks past the deserted cloakroom. Down to grace the landing whose princely staircase declined to the terrace. A speedy return, sharp left through the lobby and into the gaming rooms. Ignoring the kitchen, entering the Salons Privés where only minutes before inflated patrons were deflating their fortunes. Mural paintings turgid overhead. The long hang of dusty velvet drapes. Curves of bright

146

lamplight, angles of dim obscurity. A density to the quiet, a stunned silence to the insult of two gentlemen opening their trousers and removing short prybars from inside the legs.

Kalenberg nipped behind the nearest of two cashier cages and sprung its cash drawer. Propping his bar on the cage wicket, he took another slip out of his shirt and began scooping up the neat rows of banknotes, refusing the silver. Henri was snagging his prybar hook under the slits of the boxes built into the tables. Levering. A warpage of brass plates. A formidable splintering of black slate, polished mahogany, and inlaid rosewood. Craftsmen and carpenters spinning in their graves. Henri kept running back and forth to stuff money from each box into Kalenberg's sack. At last to stand panting by the second cage. Which Kalenberg was rifling.

'Fini, Dieter. Cleaned except for the coins and the chips.'

'We should leave a little so they can resume play.'

Jogging out again. Shoes resounding hollow along the sterile marble expanse, back around to dump their third sack on the landing. Then brushing the dust from their tuxedoes and straightening their ties, they angled across to the theatre. Henri through the left-hand entrance, Kalenberg through the middle, of meagre interest to the harried plainclothesmen shepherding the doors. To stand squashed and anonymous among the ruffled throng, who were aware the gala wasn't as it should be but not knowing why, and were pooling their ignorance with rumour and gossip. Henri smothered a grin, Kalenberg relaxing vastly serene; obviously Serault had scored a great success in the security office. His intricate mechanism had been ticking without a hitch so far – surely it would continue just as fast and smoothly.

Jennica was sitting near the middle entrance, looking depressed, baleful, her capable hands folded in her lap. She saw Kalenberg and rose to elbow her way closer to him, outwardly indifferent, giving no hint of recognition. Her fingers worked blindly with the clasp of her tiny purse, sifting inside. To squeeze the button of her miniature tone-call . . .

147

Chapter Nineteen

'No matter what I do or you do to me,' the dispatcher said, 'I can't countermand the alarm. The casino set it specifically that way.'

Marc, standing ashen, pocketed his gun. 'Let's go.'

'You won't go far. Give up,' the dispatcher said again, plumply righteous. 'Better cooperate, keep things quiet and civilized.'

Serault listened, resisting a sudden impulse. It was like the one which had prompted the dispatcher to leap and it was just as senseless, but this only added to the appeal. He had a wild urge to punch the dispatcher in the face.

'We'll warn the others,' Marc urged, 'and leave the stuff.'

'It'll go easier,' the dispatcher maintained. 'You know that.'

'I know,' Serault said, knowing he had to act promptly before he yielded to any of his impulses – surrender, flight, or hitting the dispatcher. Each tempting yet all essentially meaningless, since he was basically, irrevocably committed to Getting Out in the absolute sense used by inveterate gamblers. Jennica's call sounded at that moment. Serault hurried from the fat man to his case, to activate the transmitter signalling Talmas. Concentrating as he did: an idle remark by Ledoux now returning, other figments jelling, an idea forming . . .

Th dispatcher: 'You'll get lighter sentences if you do.'

And Marc: 'We can always try again but there's only one of us.'

148

'No, no quitting.' Serault snapped the cases. 'Our only escape is the helicopter, we knew that from the start. And since we've got to stay for it, we follow through with our original plan.'

'We can't hold out,' Marc was saying before Serault had finished.

The dispatcher was looking as if ready to blurt out what helicopter, then caught himself, pursuing his advantage. 'No helicopter can land here, and you've at most another three minutes left.'

'Before your gendarmes arrive? From where, Cap d'Ail? They'll stall in the confusion along the quai and not rip free for an hour.'

'Down from the Moyenne Corniche then, and from Cap Martin.'

'All taking more time – sufficient time for you to radio.'

The dispatcher shook his head.

Serault pounced, bunching shirt and tie in both hands, lifting the startled dispatcher. 'SBM has worked out a defence against large-scale raids, right? Logically there must be one prepared, some sort of blockade of the casino and adjacent streets.'

'So if there is?' The dispatcher truculent. 'Not another word, and no use threatening to shoot us. It's too late for you.'

'We'll operate the radio ourselves,' Marc suggested.

'Can't. He knows the procedure and they know his voice, his inflections. It has to be him. Quick, tape his wrists to the armrests.'

A brief, frantic wrestle. Serault avoided kicking feet and indecently long nails clawing at his mask. Marc fumbled for a roll of tape. The dispatcher squashed back down in his seat, cap mashed over his foolish astounded face, handkerchief sent fluttering and nose beginning to dribble again. Marc wrapped one wrist and looped the tape across to wrap the other, then down to hike his shoes off the floor, fast around the swivel plates. Cutting the tape with his knife, voilà, and Serault stepping back to ask him:

149

'Is it tight?'

'Very.'

'I hope so. I don't want him bleeding to death.'

Agitation in the chair. 'What? What?'

'Like a tourniquet. For when I slice off your fingers.'

The dispatcher lurched hopelessly, tendons straining. 'Wait –'

'Too late.' Serault held out an open palm to Marc. 'Scalpel.'

The dispatcher buckled, then reared, defiant. 'You wouldn't.'

'A poor gamble.' Serault clamped one hand flat. 'Your little finger first, I do believe. Then if you still say no – '

'Yes!' Sweating profusely, nerve crumbling. 'Morbleu, yes!'

Serault hovered over the dispatcher, a phoenix from the ashes. 'Order the blockade. Tell your outside man that a gang of thieves will be attacking disguised as French police and gendarmes.' A rude laugh from Marc; Serault ignored it, pressing on. 'Say that the fires and stuff were set as an excuse for their coming. But say not to be fooled, and to stop everything except the helicopter . . .'

The dispatcher nodding, wilting. 'Except the helicopter . . .'

'Say the helicopter is fetching a guest, the Maharaja of Greater Cojones, who's unfortunately suffered a stroke due to the excitement.'

'. . . Excitement. Now the tape, take off the tape.'

'The tape stays on. I'll work the console, you tell me how.'

'Fourth knob, turn to six . . . the two switches there go up . . .'

Serault attacked, arranging the controls. Bellying the dispatcher to the board, aligning the microphone, changing channels to view the Place. Feeling a constriction worse than any tape might cause – the squeeze of an inexorable crushing system.

The dispatcher with voice congealing: 'Attention, attention all external patrols, initiate Emergency Manoeuvre DS immediately . . .' and repeated the demands, then fell silent, sagging and darkly dismal.

Furious activity erupted, the Place glutinous with armed guards streaming in practised coordination. Erecting barricades, re-arranging old ones, slewing cruisers across intersections, fanning out and shooing civilians off the streets. The casino an island placid, appearing abandoned but well protected within a roughly semicircular perimeter. The SBM planning efficiently, yet its very precision serving the enemy equally well once inside the citadel.

A pleasing but temporary comfort, Serault fretted. As he momentarily stood watching the scene and listening to the crosstalk. Casting a fervid glance at the dispatcher then, and remembering a previous impulse. Smiling a wry, oddly satisfied smile while twirling up and around that loaded sock of his. The dispatcher shuddered, sprawling head lolling, a weary sigh trickling from his slackened mouth. The fat man fatalistic, cringing with eyes closed. And was unconscious, curled foetally as a child will do when burrowing under the bedclothes.

'Let's go,' Marc repeated, licking dry lips.

'One more thing. Where's the dispatcher's gun?'

Serault retrieved the pistol Marc had taken and began smashing the console. Breaking levers and crushing dials and mangling circuits, applying himself particularly to that damn red alarm button, which shorted out in a stink of burnt insulation. Serault lost some of his control, snarling and snapping while battering the board, the board crumpling in on itself making weird sounds like the groanings of torment. Retaliating with spits and fizzles but Serault undaunted waded into the metal. A fatal haemorrhage, the moorings wrenching loose. Wire flying, parts falling, speaker mute and screens blank, the console collapsed and died.

Serault dropped the useless bent revolver and, huffing softly, retrieved his attaché case and headed for the door. '*Now* we'll go.'

Outside and down the corridor. Marc first in case they were glimpsed, a guard more orthodox than a gorilla. Swivelling to ponder Serault with question and awe. 'A devastating trump back there, brilliantly improvised. But René, would you have?'

'No names, ever.'

'Sorry. But would you have actually cut off his fingers?'

Serault stroked up under the mask where his neck was aching. 'I don't know,' he said slowly. Dismissing a twinge of conscience that had seeped in and keeping his features coldly objective. 'I really don't know. It was bad luck the situation arose at all, and good luck we didn't have to face it. Let's leave it at that.'

Hastening on. The gorilla finding himself unable to leave it at that, too acutely aware how suddenly his plans and portents had deteriorated in a spasm of fate . . . Luck was the axis. And when depending on luck, there were those who had it all and those who had none. And those like himself whose luck paraded in drag . . .

Chapter Twenty

Wesley Talmas gathered against the crane. 'Mrs Ledoux – '

'Fifine, remember?' Closing in.

'Nothing's the matter, Fi – ' Clogging on her name, raising an arm between them to tap his watch. The time seemed unchanged; he wondered peripherally if he'd forgotten to wind it. 'But I swore I heard something else than cats. And it's very, very late.'

'Never too late.' She pushed down his arm, English accent a gumbo in his ear. 'Or too little. Plenty of time to enjoy ourselves.'

Talmas tried squeezing from underneath, moaning faintly from the weight of her insistent girth. Sensing the spectacular confrontation she was brewing and mentally scurrying for shelter. 'I enjoy . . . enjoyment as much as any man, but I . . . I'm working now.'

'Not hard enough.'

'I'm working with Bernard. Don't forget your husband.'

'My husband doesn't understand me.' She bowed her head, placing her hands on his chest. 'And I don't understand him.' Pushing suddenly as if resisting his advances, leaving Talmas breathless to straighten, coquettish, pouting. 'Bernard's up to no good. You all are. I don't know what it is, but I know it's no good.'

'No –'

'It's so obvious. All your skulking and secret meetings.'

'No such thing, I assure – '

'I wonder if the police know,' she added lightly, eyes

153

shrouded and sly. Kicking off scruffy carpet slippers to pose on her toes like a ballerina. 'Why, and you act as if I'm not enough for you.'

'Dear sweet Jesus,' Talmas said very gently.

'Silly man, you probably think you prefer those skinny girls with ribs you can count at a distance.' She was smiling, lips parted and teeth glinting. 'With lemon breasts and pinched faces. Good only for making bruises, believe me, and – what's that?'

That: a doorbell ringing in the cockpit of the helicopter.

Talmas, already eroded, giving a little yip of surprise. Pulse violent, determined to sweep together the remnants of his courage and find some means of pacifying this woman. Other than the obvious method she was pursuing. He stammered:

'I – I have to go. Go now.'

'Don't be absurd. Isn't the moonlight divine tonight?'

'But I must.'

'Would you like me to undress in the moonlight?'

'Mrs – Fi – I mean, I've been signalled.'

Her breath loud and adoring. 'Dear man, you've been summoned.'

Talmas could only crouch on the running board, feeling a fibre inside him breaking like the first strand of a frayed cord. Staring glazed while Madame Ledoux unbuttoned her peignoir. Widening her gown, exposing a swathe of pale flesh, then gradually letting it slide. Down kettle breasts and a cauldron belly, over hips of hamhock and legs of mutton, off to puddle around her feet. She stepped free and closer, knuckles resting on thighs and legs spread wide. Amazonian thicket poised. 'Have me,' she whispered.

'A misunderstand – '

'Have me or the cops.'

'Please, you're not serious.'

'I am, dear man.' Pirouetting, gazing about the yard. 'Where? Not on the ground; too dirty and hard.' Mincing a few steps to the wreckage of a four-door sedan. Tugging on its rear handle, the door buckled and only coming open after

154

determined insistence. She leaned in to check the coils of its wide seat with expectant thumpings. 'Oh lovely. Get undressed, oh hurry, hurry.'

Talmas paralysed with his back to the crane, conscious of more strands giving internally. Watching the rolling dunes of her buttocks as she ducked further, crawling in, her voice funnelling out to him: 'You can't enjoy with your clothes on, can you?'

'Look, you're trying to pay Bernard back for some reason, but –'

'Make up your mind. Either you come to me or I go to the cops.' From the black depths her hand uncoiled, making a pantomime of milking in the dreary air. 'You won't be sorry. I'll show you a little speciality that made me famous all the way up to Strasbourg.'

The final strand parted deep within Talmas.

Pure horror activated him now. Launching him springing, rushing the car, his shoulder ramming the door. Jamming it shut on tortured hinges. If he climbed in that rear seat he'd be swallowed alive. Devoured. The only leftovers some entrails maybe and his prick, found infected with prostratis by then he was sure.

A spiralling scream, Madame Ledoux scrabbling with hands and face against the glass. While Talmas rebounded from the impact and leaped for the crane. He'd been scared for weeks – scared that Serault's wild theories would work and then scared they wouldn't; scared of the preparations and of the actual operation; scared for himself and for the others. But never before had he experienced awesome horror. Into the driver's seat, grinding the starter, the motor coughing, eventually catching. Foot nursing the throttle, Talmas studying the maze of controls with the genius of a man knowing he doesn't have time to learn but knowing he must anyway. Thrusting, yanking. The antique limousine resisting, but gradually turning. The jib slowly lowering – no, the other lever – rising and rotating over the sedan. The crab gyrating, Talmas experimenting, the massive claws opening and closing the way Madame Ledoux had beckoned from the rear seat. Then dropping tenderly but quickly, Talmas not wishing to harm her but fearing her rabid attempts to get free would be in time.

'I'm sorry,' he yelled. 'I'm sorry to have to do this.'

His expression of regret and necessity were lost in the clatter of cylinders and her shrill bellows of outrage. The crab scraping across the rusted roof, hooks clinging to the rim. Daintily closing to take a gargantuan bite. Talmas reversing a lever, engaging a clutch. The talon gripping harder, raising the sedan with a crumpling and shattering. The load suddenly shifting, her great naked bulk meeting the front seat, smothering it, and shoving it forward. Producing yet another howl for this unspeakable assault. Talmas correcting, restoring the balance if not the tranquillity of Madame Ledoux. Winding cables and erecting the jib, watching the car swaying first one way then the other like a pendulum. Safely curled in the crab ten metres off the ground. Too far for her to jump.

Talmas set the levers and cut the ignition, stumbling with guilt to the helicopter, where in the plexiglass he caught his reflection, hectic and dismayed. Averting his face, he fired the turbine and cinched the seat belt too tight against the cold that was knotting in his stomach. Lifting off, he came level with the car, and, ashamed, he feathered the pitch to move closer beside it.

'Please try to understand,' he cried out. 'It's not personal . . .'

He trailed off, realizing the futility. Madame Ledoux was tossing her head, vast coral mouth agape, wailing with increasing incoherence. Her seduction had been spurned and was recoiling to her loins, where in that thick jungle her lust would burn with vindictive appetite. She was in no mood for apologies, now or ever.

Still she couldn't stay hooked indefinitely; what would she do once Bernard winched her down? A problem of nightmarish dimension and potential, but to be solved later, later. Now Talmas ascended in an easy curve, pulling himself together to meet the more immediate future, sloping towards

156

Monte Carlo and contemplating the tangle of terrace decorations that would undoubtedly be fouling his landing. The wrecking yard, crane, and Madame Ledoux faded beneath and behind ...

Chapter Twenty-One

The Principality was floundering, ensnarled in an atmosphere of smog and ferment: the firemen penetrating police headquarters, deluging the basement to keep the blaze from cars not already consumed; the other shifts of Sûreté Publique arriving, and from the Rock a contingent of Palace Guards descending: to help restore harmony and hold at bay the rapidly swelling number of curious. Mainly hampering, further congesting the Quai, Boulevard Albert 1er, and surrounding streets.

Up on Boulevard Princess Alice the fire was more or less under control, having burnt itself out in the smaller enclosure, the walls made of brick and stone, sooty but little damaged. Though the flames had licked up through the garage ceiling, fusing the wires and melting the transceiver. The burst van had been found, causing considerable speculation. The firemen at the substation radioed their dispatcher, who in turn radioed Nice and discovered the casino had beaten their distress alarm by a few minutes. And indeed, gazing up Princess Alice, they could see a cordon being organized on Avenue des Beaux-Arts against some mysterious but manifestly dangerous threat.

SMB guards were prowling around barricades and hunching in cruisers, automatic weapons near at hand. The Café de Paris was closing, its customers flushed outside, told to go home and shutter the windows. The lobby of the Hôtel clearing, guests escorted upstairs and ordered to keep their rooms dark. In all the turbulence and consternation, with the

158

twin distractions of fires and entrenchments, the sheets draping the Horsten display were never questioned. The strange new pantry door in the Empire Room was overlooked. The quarantine sign hanging across the men's room was assumed to be Gospel, those regarding it stepping by with haste and ginger. The few who noticed the absence of the manager and concierge were ignored, the official defenders preoccupied, their attentions directed outwards.

Sentried just up from the Place were Alphonse and Gaston, behind a hastily fabricated wooden barrier blocking Avenue de la Madone, almost at an intersection of Avenue de Grande-Bretagne. The cocktail garden of the old hotel Metropole on their right, a deep excavation for an impending apartment complex kitty-corner, and the preciously landscaped Boulingrine stretching along their left. Sitting fidgety on their heels. Checking their pistols. Baffled by the abrupt and unexplained silence from the casino, but focusing their concern on the imminent assault. Shifting occasionally to limber their legs, or when another site seemed to offer more shelter. To check their pistols some more. Squatting again.

'What d'you think?' Gaston whispered, though there was no need.

'I don't know. What do you think?'

'I think it makes sense now, what's been happening tonight.'

'We're lucky to've found out in time.'

Gaston produced a small flat bottle of cognac from his jacket, breaking its seal. 'I'm curious to know who they really are.'

'We'll learn soon enough.' Alphonse peered forlornly ahead, then, spying his partner, 'Ah! Pass it here, you're a comrade for life.'

'Not so fast. If you want a drink, it's only to the first star.'

The first star on the label graced the bottle neck, allowing a thimble's worth of cognac. Grimacing, Alphonse snatched the bottle and opened it, swallowing until the level fell to the brand name.

'You guzzler, don't drink it all.'

159

'Almost made me drop it, you did.' Reproachfully swigging again before handing the bottle back. 'French, I bet. They'll turn out to be French, I'm positive of it.'

'Sneaky enough.' Gaston himself nipped at the cognac.

'Deplorable, dressing up as police.'

'Insidious. Here, the last is yours.'

'I'm surprised the ruse wasn't thought of before.' Alphonse scrutinized the empty bottle for clinging drops. Then frowned. Then pitched the bottle at Gaston. 'That was *my* cognac!'

'They're coming.' Gaston backing away. 'I hear them coming.'

'Lying won't help you. You filched that bottle out of my locker and I'm going to – 'Alphonse stopped, staring up the Avenue, where the bray of sirens was growing from a distant mist to a deafening blanket of sound. 'You're right, they are.' Dodging below the barrier, cocking his pistol, the quicksilver shrieking plummeting closer. 'But you wait, Gaston, until this is over . . .'

An invasion of gendarmes cornered on Boulevard des Moulins, careering down Avenue de la Madone. Clouds of dust and smoke from tyres rising dervishly around the sedans, Black Marias, and *motards* on their cycles. 'They've even painted their cars to trick us,' Gaston roared. The lead car, a blue Renault, ran over one of the spikes Ledoux had frantically sprinkled on the roadway; its left front tyre exploded.

'They're shooting at us, Gaston!'

The driver lost control. Heeling, leaving a fat stroke of rubber, creaming into the side of a Lamborghini belonging to a German from West Berlin who'd travelled expressly for the gala.

'We got him, Gaston, we got him!'

Gaston, perplexed, glancing about. 'Who did?'

Abreast of the car, the first motard attempted evasion. Overcompensating, dipping between the two rows of parked cars lining the Avenue and splintering the fence protecting the excavation. Driving full throttle down the slope, kicking up sparklers of gravel and rock. A beige sedan fishtailing, striking the blue Renault at an angle. Brakes locked, a cumbrous Black Maria van swerving into all three, mashing beige into blue and wedging the Lamborghini up against a fire hydrant. Which fractured, producing a geyser. A second motorcycle sent spinning by the suddenly wet pavement, rearing and plunging straight along Avenue Grande-Bretagne. The wild-eyed motard clutching its saddle, the rest of him straddling its rear fender.

'So! Barricades are to be ignored!' Gaston straightening, pointing accusingly at the cyclist. 'Now they're trying side streets!'

Alphonse glared. 'Diversionary tactics won't help them.'

More sedans. Hitting spikes. Veering right and left. Skidding perpendicular and bouncing down the stairs of the Metropole garden. Shattering glass-topped tables and squashing wrought-iron chairs. Stampeding the foolish guests who'd assembled in jaded interest at the entrance. Collapsing the outdoor cocktail booth, winding in and blinded by the striped canvas of the booth's awning. Others leaping into the Boulingrins. Flattening shrubs, hedges, beds of flowers and a small orchard of young palms. Ploughing ruttishly through a sunken garden the Principality had lavished a decade to perfect. Steaming, sinking to the hub caps in the muck of lily and reed ponds.

Alphonse dizzy. 'They're branching out, surrounding us.'

Gaston raging. 'Don't let them past, remember our orders.'

Behind the pack as if urging them on, a black Peugot 404 station wagon boiled around the curve, tyres screaming. A four-wheel drifting. Straight for the barrier. Both guards ogling the onrushing slab, forgetting all vows as they leaped low, a profile huddling as one. The Peugot stopped – ceased – with a pulverizing collision, thunder reverberating heavy in their ears. Planks rising up and away, chrome raking against sawhorses and diminishing them to shavings. Kindling raining on the body accordioned now, frame sprung, glass cracked. Wisps percolating from the hood.

Gaston probed, found his partner. 'Are you all right?'

161

'Don't paw me, I'm fine. Not that you'd light a candle if my back were broken.' Alphonse stumbled upright, waving a hand to clear the air. 'Is he alive? Where'd he go?'

The driver was already out of his Peugot. A huge white-haired man in torn epaulettes and battered képi, utterly ignoring Gaston and Alphonse. Hacking and lurching and ranting back up the Avenue, brandishing his steering wheel.

Alphonse raised his pistol. 'We'll at least capture that one.'

'Hold it,' Gaston swatting Alphonse's arm. 'Listen.'

Something about malloz-ru, you vauriens, move your fesses and fall in toute suite. And from the Boulingrins, hotel garden, excavation and vehicular debris were coming a dozen or so gendarmes. Limping, cursing, dragging truncheons and selves.

Alphonse listening, giddy. 'But he sounds . . . They act so . . .'

'Exactly.'

'Gaston, I think they're authentic. I think we've been deceived.'

'Alphonse?' Gaston shagging black eyebrows at the serried gendarmes, the ruptured barrier, then back towards the casino. 'Alphonse,' he said in tones viscid, 'I think we've been *had*.'

162

Chapter Twenty-Two

Serault and Marc reached the main lobby.

Separating, Marc drifted inside the northern, side entrance of La Salle Garnier to linger behind two plainclothesmen. Clasping hands at his back and flexing his shoes, looking pompous as only stolid men of bulk and uniform can look. Listening absently to the babble and the orchestra, while keeping his eyes fixed upon the Royal Box that protruded over the middle of the small theatre.

Serault scudded along to the Prince's staircase: through the curtain, seeing three bloated pillowcases propped against the landing wall. Excellent. Dieter and Henri had evidently executed an exquisite rape; a stunning thrust, rooting thoroughly to withdraw rapidly before they were noticed much less protested.

Swiftly up the private steps, Serault gripped by emotions abrasive with anticipation and dread. Ahead lay his raison d'être, the spore from which his hydra-headed scheme had bloomed – the jewels of the Red Cross Gala. Most notably his own necklace – or rather, what was left of it. Yet conditions had degenerated, distinctly menacing if not downright exterminating. Still, he'd tackled that unforeseeable blunder in the security office with nimble ingenuity, to his credit whatever the outcome. Even if the whole damn mess went straight down.

Into the grotesque plush box, leaning over its brass rail. Suspended between laurel-wreathed gods and lyre-plucking maids plastered above, and the often more florid gentility

163

and faded *noctambules* seated below. As programmed, Marc was to the side, Henri by the left, and Kalenberg and Jennica positioned at the middle door. Serault forced to cover the stage wings from his vantage, its exit left precariously unlocked due to their lack of manpower. Mordieu, if only those Stens could've been finagled inside as Marc had desired. Pistols would suffice to deter the sane, but nobody could predict musicians: who, for reasons known only to themselves, were currently foxtrotting with *Glow-worm*.

And who, since they were facing the captive audience, were the first to spot the gorilla standing in the Royal Box. Their melody withered. Leaking notes and shedding bars, the already insecure chorus deflating. The audience craning about and then up, to gape with avid curiosity. As if expecting the gorilla to be part of some scandalous extravaganza being performed for their amusement.

In unison: Serault raised his gun in a high, wide arc.

Kalenberg with meaty arm backed Jennica against the door pillar.

Jennica screamed.

A superb contralto of compass and depth, nasally pitched in the higher octaves perhaps, yet formidably sustaining. Causing an immediate reaction of wonder and alarm. Impressing Serault, who realized she wasn't merely pretending; she was genuinely afraid. The echoes of her scream still vibrated as he said loudly:

'Don't move. Anybody, anybody at all, moves and we kill her.'

Pausing. Needing a moment for his warning to sink in. But tense against spontaneity, worried that personnel who lived by the gun would instinctively assume he should die by it. They'd been trained well, however, in the savagery of pistols fired at close range. Paling, souring, yet stymied, the staff did not challenge.

Instead, a slender nonentity broke during that frozen instant. 'Help, oh dear me!' A panicked adagio for the left door, elegant wrists aflutter in velvet cuffs, lace ruffle dancing on a magenta shirt. Henri waited. A leisurely backhand, the

164

barrel gleaming. The man peeping, falling back to disappear.

Serault now calling: 'We're everywhere, at the doors and outside. You can't escape; we'll kill the next one who tries.' And without pausing he gestured towards Marc. 'You, the baby hippo.'

'Me?' Marc truly surprised, not expecting the endearment.

'Collect the weapons and don't forget your own. Quick!'

'Foutre!' Marc, stung, muttered back, advancing to the two plainclothesmen and taking off his cap to form a basket. 'God knows how many there are,' he told them. 'We better go along.'

Sullen, they slid automatics from their shoulder-holsters.

'No more?' Marc asked as they placed them in his cap.

'I've an MAB .32 on my belt,' one confided.

Marc, with a defeatist shrug: 'A toy. What if it were found? And think of the guests. Their welfare is our main responsibility.'

The man sighed, taking out his second gun.

While from the box Serault was commanding: 'The rest of you, start removing your valuables. Money, jewels – everything. And if we find you're hiding anything, we'll shoot you where you sit.'

His resurgent voice, viscous and adamant. The tearful hostage, whimpering helplessly. The brutal guns, one pressing up under her throat. The slim gentleman now petulantly sobbing. The malevolent gorilla lording overhead. Intimidation was complete.

'But you won't be hurt if you obey,' Serault kept on, knowing he must pace fast and relentless, prodding with threats and nudging with guns to keep them on the defensive. And mistrusting their gritty quiet, their mutinous hush. He aimed at the stage, demanding: 'Music, some music.'

The orchestra stirred feebly, remaining silent, until an elderly viola player who'd traditionally plied British cruise ships launched into the first tune he could recall: *Nearer My God To Thee.*

The desperate and mournful quavers accompanied Henri, who was passing down the aisles. Having unfurled the last

165

three pillowslips from his shirt, and leaving two beside the door, he was holding the third wide and jiggling it impatiently. Teeth bared back. Intermittently growling. Occasionally lunging as if to rip off some bauble. Shaking down the cowering guests as fiercely as he could.

Marc continued harvesting the beefstock sulky in their tuxedoes and uniforms. The majority sheepish but obedient, the couple of holdouts cajoled and disarmed after a few discouraging words. Arriving midway he said, 'I hate this,' to a guard of savage countenance, 'but we don't have much choice, really.'

'No? While I bring up my gun,' the guard said, working the flap of his holster, 'you act like you're taking it from me.'

Marc beside the guard felt his draw. Reflexively he wedged his hand between to push the revolver back into its holster. The hammer punching the web of his thumb and forefinger, the guard having spastically pulled the trigger. And now he was glaring with puzzlement.

'Consider.' Marc gasping, vision blurring from the pain. 'A robbery is embarrassing, but we'd never live down dead patrons.'

'There won't be a massacre. Pop the leader, the rest will fold.'

'You can't be sure. Consider the girl if nobody else.'

'One shot. All I want, one shot at that *cocotte* up there.'

'She'd certainly be killed. And it'd be just our luck if she's a highness or the mistress to a prime minister. Mon ami, consider.'

The guard considered . . . Then grudgingly eased on the hammer.

'We'll get them later,' Marc said, masking relief, feeling blood warm in his palm as he took the revolver. 'Later, you'll see . . .' Shuttling on before the guard reconsidered or more time was wasted. His bundle of weapons growing until it required both hands to carry.

Serault ordering when he was done: 'Load them in the sack lying at the left exit. Then take the other sack and help my man.'

Marc readily complying. Still shaken by his trim with the guard, his hand smarting and sticky. Cautioning those near the exit: 'Don't mess with the guns.' Then cracking the door just wide and long enough to shove through the sack of weapons. 'Sacre! Another ten armed men outside. We mustn't take any risks.' He snatched up the bag, gathering their belongings. The group were convinced his agitation was from anger and regard for their safety as he joined his brother in looting the stalls.

Serault surveyed the sacking, the literal sacking of the Red Cross Gala, seized by an excitement blended with satisfactions and regrets. Sensing the cold fury of Nicole Hibou when Henri approached – ice throughout except in her cheeks which were burning a slow and livid colour; and in her eyes when she surrendered the necklace, widening as if in pain, in actual agony. Serault regretted he could not personally have bagged it. And also regretted that Nicole at least could not learn who and why. But impossible. These regrets minor compared to the satisfaction of:

Watches, earrings, bracelets, wallets, purses, brooches. Onyx and coral and lapiz lazuli. Floral, bow, and ribbon motifs. Silver and platinum, yellow and white gold settings. Emeralds and rubies and pearls and diamonds, oh the diamonds of rose, brilliant, and marquise cuts. The Vattiers like efficient deacons gliding along pews. Their trapped congregation faintly stirring despite their terror, inherently indignant at so stupendous a tithe. At being plucked so naked, left with nothing but prayers for retribution.

Serault felt their simmerings, breathing easier when the collection was finally over. 'We're going,' he told them. 'But we're taking the girl and the guard with us, as insurance.'

Marc and Henri under bulky pillowslips, charging the left exit. Crashing through without slowing. Kalenberg carefully backing out of the middle door, his wriggling shield shrinking from his gun and hence closer to him. Protecting his wider flank. A collective sigh once in the hall, doors closed. Marc grabbing the sack of guns, all of them sprinting for the landing. Where Henri took his sack from Van Cleef's and

Kalenberg picked up his plus the one from the Salons Privés. Jennica running, the three men lumbering from their double loads, down the stairs and out onto the terrace.

Where far by the balcony the copter was idling.

Still in the Royal Box, Serault was hesitating, allowing the others time, nervously studying for signs of weapons and potential martyrdom. 'Remember, the girl and the guard are with us. They'll be released unharmed when we're safe.' Unsure those below believed or even cared about any of this any longer. Smelling their resentments, the rising vapour seething and ugly: 'If you try to stop us – if there's any trouble at all – they'll be the first to die.'

Retreating then with a sweep of his gun. Down the steps two at a time, clutching his attaché case, to the landing –

– Hearing voices and feet converging –

– Plunging down more steps. Not looking back. If this ended in a spineful of lead, it was too late to prevent it. His power had slipped badly; he'd sensed his hold over the masses critically declining, possibly decaying beyond the control of any one man. But he'd got out as soon as he could. His only hope now lay in taking the stairs as quickly as he could without breaking a leg.

Alarmed shoutings, cries for reinforcements, converging sirens incited him on, to the terrace, while behind him an SBM guard was frothing about Gaston and it's a gorilla and halt. Halt or I'll fire.

A pistol coughed. A bullet furrowed the scalp of his mask.

Chapter Twenty-Three

Flight.

An erratic zigzag across the festive no-man's land. Towards the threshing helicopter where arms were strained urging. Lungs burning. Eyes watering. The tiles chiselling and grit spraying, powder stinging from bullets stitching, overtaking. Serault veering, impulsively seeking the nearest shelter. An obese Ali Baba urn potted with shrub, the leafy bush cushioning his impact. Roots precariously anchored, sucking loose, Serault and foliage sailing together and bowling over the urn. Smashing it, shards and damp soil.

To flatten behind. While groping open his attaché case, scrounging inside for the last of the plastique. Serault's palms and the lengths between his fingers clammy as he jammed in and snapped off a time-fuse pencil. Then he sent the case skittering away unnoticed in the clamour, under the bunting and among the pilings of giant pink seashell bandstand.

Serault held his breath, feeling peculiarly disembodied as if hovering over the terrace, watching guards spilling down the steps, firing enthusiastically. And guests trailing after in growing number, bristling from the scent of revenge and retrieval. Able to reconcile pestilence, slaughter, rape of their women – but not theft. Theft steals their means to buy a way out. And himself, cringing under his impromptu Maginot of shedding leaves and flaking pottery. Depending on a tiny morsel of explosive insufficient for a respectable fart. The one or three seconds becoming taffy, stretching eternally . . .

A blast thick and rasping. The stage shuddered.

The shooting lapsed while everyone stared at it.

Serault already on his feet in an ungainly dash. A dullish pain of failure in his chest, glancing at the mob reviving. Swarming forward, refusing to stay back but mingling with the guards and jostling their aim. Remorselessly pursuing.

Two more blasts, louder, ruffling the banners and trembling the shell. A furry tongue of flames licking outwards, more sprouting instantly to ring the stage. Disconcerting the mob. Some retreating, those at the rear still advancing, a few in the middle trampled inbetween and shouting about it, more startled than hurt. A guard still charging unretarded, obstinately yelling and waving his pistol.

Serault glimpsed obliquely, heard vaguely *that* guard, the one who'd parted his hair with a bullet. Abruptly swivelling to crouch on one knee, sighting his automatic with his arm locked – a foolhardy tactic he'd once seen in a western movie otherwise worth forgetting. The guard lurching, caught unaware with gun dangling. Disjointedly waltzing, eyes aching on Serault who was squeezing the trigger, then chucking his own gun over his shoulder. Bleakly flinching. Serault wavered . . . pivoted, up and running. To concentrate solely on his finishing spurt. Ignoring the guard. Oblivious of the orders, the countermands, the crowd resurging maddened and disoriented. Uncaring that fire had blossomed up to ignite the pink shell, hungrily consuming sashes, streamers, and flags.

Reaching the hatch. Clutching at hands, vaulting among the four crammed together to lift him in. Rolling against Jennica, usually soft but now impermeable with a lapful of guns. Kalenberg's glasses broken, Marc with his wig awry, Henri with his shirt-front curling like a windowshade. Talmas at his seat hunching over the controls.

An instant. Perched on the terrace, turbine whining, blades clattering, hopes fading. The crowd too close, roaring and swamping, having lost any semblance of propriety or caution. The next instant straight up. No curving, no taxing, simply straight up.

Serault wheezing against the compression. Hearing the

170

suckings of the others, the faint gaspings from Jennica mashed underneath him, her dress being ripped by the guns. Viewing through a blur the diminishing terrace, the shrivelling clot of milling guests and guards. The shrinking bandstand creaking and moaning as if in orgasm – then suddenly expanding, unexpectedly glowing. A phosporescence sizzling out from it, punching a hole in the fishnet and erupting with a technicolor spangle.

A second rocket right behind, ricocheting off the trident and arcing past the copter in a deafening cascade of strontium red. The trident buckling, the bandstand sagging. The crowds dodging and dancing, suddenly counfounded by a rash of whirlygigs razzling among them. The blaze creating a vortex of its own, buoying the fishnet as it broke free. The sprawling web unfolding, floating down in a sequined flood. There were yells as some saw it, one man retiring under a table and to hell with his squealing wife. Most thrashed against the enmeshing cloak, fouling and snaring, falling incoherently in on themselves and the exploding fireworks.

Serault stared amazed. His idea had been one diversionary bang, a feeble one at that; the fire had been an extra and gratefully used. But he'd forgotten if he'd ever known the display was under the stage. The result unplanned – nothing this spectacular could've been. The scattered confusions of the tangled herd had now coalesced into a single mindless swaying of the net. Weaving and pitching in response to the fireworks pouring into it varied and profuse. Starclusters twirling, windmills tilting, dragonflies wriggling and lashing their tails. Meteors, tornadoes and galaxies discharging, quivering the terrace and rattling the casino.

'Alphonse, they're flying away,' one guard cried. But no one noticed Gaston, including his partner. The net flung itself forwards at a chorus of white whistlers. To be repulsed by a luxuriant fizzjigger bathing the net in copper blue, sodium yellow, and barium green. Which in the sky would have flared wide to show the Passion of St Agnostes. Tables overturning, chairs folding, platters and bottles dragged underfoot. The net encompassing them all like an amoeba,

171

streaming self and possessions around in eddies and whirls. Trying to elude and escape but going nowhere. A recirculating Joad's odyssey swelling and floundering amid groans and wails . . .

. . . Meanwhile the copter had been turning. Sharply canting, piling everybody into a solid mass. Kalenberg raving. 'Stop this!'

Talmas, cemented in his posture: 'Are we safe or dead?'

'A moot point. Slow down and we may discover.'

Talmas swung the copter horizontal but continued accelerating. Running parallel with the coastline, only a few dim lamps beading the hillside. Wind soughing. Moon dappling a sea gently lapping. A generous night of darkness, calm. Except behind them, which was incandescent and shivering from merry detonations.

'Get off me,' Jennica panted. Serault obliged, helping to shift the pillowcases to the rear and two duffle bags forward. Jennica unzipped her dress, splitting it like a carcase, shedding it and her bra; while the men were undressing, cutting and ripping all clothes and costumes into strips and stuffing them in one bag. Taking from the second make-up removers, solvents, rags, and a kit with a lighted mirror for Jennica, who was wearing just tights. Casually delicate about it, Serault thought, himself only in underwear. So studiously indifferent as she began winding a bandage around to level her breasts. Conscious of being watched yet not even shyness to show she was aware. You pretend well, chérie, but be careful of wolves in the audience . . .

The copter passed inland, avoiding Menton's lights as much as possible, though they were a tracery of mainly deserted streets.

Marc was cleaning his face. 'It almost soured on us.'

Kalenberg, queasily: 'It's still not over, not till we land.'

'Not even then.' Talmas morose, sloping towards the Carei valley.

'But almost.' Henri euphoric. 'You've the wrong altitude.'

'I get it up when I have to.' Talmas misunderstanding, scanning the familiar terrain but unable to identify Ledoux's

172

yard. 'I don't mean sexually and I don't mean taking off from the terrace.'

'Like jet emulsion,' Henri cut in. Derailing a rickety train of thoughts, sending Talmas blurting, groping for words:

'Listen, you've got to know. What I mean is Mrs Ledoux suspects what we've done. What we're doing. She's threatened to go to the cops. She's quite liable to if she gets down out of the car.'

Serault leaned forward, almost afraid to ask: 'What car?'

'I hoisted it with the crane but fast. Fast right up. The other takes half an hour, you see, even when I work at it. I must be delirious, I've got to cut this before it all falls apart. There were circumstances I'll discuss alone with Bernard. I did what I could.'

Serault sat back, rubbing his neck, the group tightening in stunned quietude as he considered: Bernard, wife, probable circumstances best left private, what to say if anything to his crumbling pilot . . . 'I'm sure you did,' he sighed at last. 'Please, Wesley, perk up. Nothing more can be done until we see Bernard, and besides, it won't be our problem then but his. Has been, I believe; he's mentioned things in the past. Enough. Will somebody pass me my socks . . . ?'

The men putting on rumpled shirts, filthy coveralls, stained work gloves and mud-caked boots. Talmas already that way. Jennica dressing similarly after applying pan-stiks and liners and a shaggy brown wig, to appear younger. But as a boy, an apprentice to these grubby labourers. The copter hugged contours sparsely wooded, patched with weedy fields and isolated *cabanons*. It approached the quarry. They could begin to see the barren grey maw opening from the forest. Closer, and the steep slopes became apparent, blueing in the moonlight. Then the blackness of the pit, corrugated with gravel and stubbled gorse. The copter slanting, Talmas looking grimly petrified.

'If only Bernard were here,' Kalenberg groaned from inside his coat where he'd wrapped his head like a tortoise withdrawing.

'Shut up.' Talmas tenacious at the controls, determined to

vindicate himself. 'If I can lift his wife, I can damn well lower this machine.' An angular dive, the copter fluttering and bobbing until Talmas judged he was positioned. Then planing, skids jarring across uneven ground, coming to a tilter rest. Beside two Mercedes-Benz diesels, a dump truck and a cement mixer, both dusty beige with their SBM logos masked by phoney nameplates.

Climbing out. Immediately the Vattiers started lugging the duffle bags towards the mixer. Serault and Talmas hauled pillowcases after them, waiting to climb on the rear and feed contents into the hopper. Jennica remained in the copter to hand down more sacks, doublechecking for any stray bits that could betray them if found later. And Kalenberg hustling for a nearby clump of boulders.

'What's wrong?' Talmas yelled. 'It was a good flight.'

'Any flight I'm alive after is a good flight.' Kalenberg disappeared among the niches. The sounds of retching.

Serault called to him: 'Check on Roche while you're out there.'

Henri took another sack to the mixer, Talmas wrestling the one full of guns, Marc arranging the empty sacks and duffle bags in the dump-truck bed, jumping down to head for its cap. Serault returning with the last sack, breathing deeply of the quarry. Enjoying the stone and bracken. The jagged cliffs and surrounding fir forest. The murmurs of the Nieya River.

The sighs of Kalenberg feeling better. 'Ach, I loathe flying.'

Talmas, aggrieving: 'Drink beforehand since it bothers you.'

'Liquor only sharpens my sense of mortality, so it wouldn't help me – Help! Mein Gott, the rope's here but the boy is gone!'

'Roche? Where?'

'René, you dolt, what do you mean *where*? Anywhere!'

The moon flowed solemn over the uneven crater. And eyes were glowing from the small animals burrowing in the crevices, any pair potentially Roche's, thought Serault as

174

he gazed slowly around. This was a numbing shock, like some bad dream Talmas might've conjured.

'He's not got far,' Marc said low and hopeful, running to help Kalenberg search the darkness. 'Not him in those tight trousers and thin shoes.' Emphatic, he thrashed kicking at some brushwood.

From the other side of the bush came an ear-piercing shriek.

Chapter Twenty-Four

Marc reared apoplectic. 'Out of there, the both of you!'

Ginette Vattier, hair awry and cotton dress askew. Scrambling from the brush, fragmenting explanations. 'All my fault – overheard you once about the quarry – planning something dreadful for tonight – drive the old Simca here to stop you – poor Fernand tied and gagged – hid the car, hid here afraid you'd hurt, you wouldn't listen –'

Marc not listening, only reaching. Roche came soaring while trying to tuck in his shirt-tails. 'I know how this must look sir – '

'You're right.' Marc swinging a massive clout, but Roche was still in motion and it passed by his doughy face. Roche twirling anyway and pedalled back into the brush. Ginette leaping in between, hoping to hold her brother and embrace Roche at the same time. 'Don't you dare hit Fernand again, you're tearing my heart out!'

'I'll tear his head off.'

Henri by this time at his brother's side. 'They're engaged.'

Marc froze, the notion trickling through. 'Engaged . . .'

A lot of white was growing in Roche's eyes. 'Oui?' He rolled the word like a candy, savouring its flavour. 'Oui . . . At first sight, almost. After we'd been talking. A quick decision, some might even say hasty, but I'm for prompt action. For seizing opportunities.'

'Seizing, were you!' Marc cocked his fist.

'Wait.' Serault retaining Marc. 'He could've run away.'

'I could've. I could've tricked her into untying me and then

176

taken her car.' Roche glanced at Ginette modestly stretching the wrinkles out of her dress. Back at Marc to wheedle. 'But I grasped there was more to gain by ah, waiting with her for you. So I didn't. Just like I didn't see two diesel trucks or the faces of six workmen if the police should ask.'

'Which they will shortly.' Serault patting dust from Roche's shirt. 'We've underestimated you, I do believe. A man of action, of opportunities. Who's seen instead four men in tuxedoes, correct?'

Marc frowning, leery of Roche's nodding. 'Can we trust you?'

'Sir, my pledge is worthy of trust . . . and of invest-ment.'

'A-hah!' Marc raised his arms and Ginette made a plain-tive cry, but he only clasped Roche to him, kissing both cheeks. 'Brother!'

Next Henri. The rest crowding around, congratulating, advising.

'They were holding a lady and a guard as hostages,' Talmas said.

'Ja.' Kalenberg beaming. 'Und driving big black limou-sines.'

Jennica shaking hands. 'Talking of the Col de Tende route.'

'Escaping into Italy,' Serault added, 'which may likely spark a government confrontation, assuming Rome hasn't dissolved again by tomorrow. And assuming we're not still here by tomorrow.'

'Eh, the time – ' Marc pointing to Ginette: 'Tie him up and get back home.' To Roche: 'You'll soon know why you've made a wise choice.' Then to the trucks, elephantine with pride.

Marc leading in the mixer, Serault and Jennica bracing against the jolts, Henri driving the dumptruck with Kalen-berg and Talmas. Leaving Roche clasping Ginette, nostrils snuffling the crown of her head. And Ginette a cameo of love in the moonlight. Or of resignation, considering the similar natures of her fiancé and brothers . . .

Up twin ruts among scrub and shale, creeping in com-

177

pound-low gear. Topping the quarry and into the dense forest, pitching eight kilometres over a meandrous washboard imprinted with lizards and snails. Bouncing onto the main highway, springs complaining. Not speeding, but respectably, innocently slow. Into Sospel, winding from the intersection through slim lanes, and out, once again on the road to Menton. Marc talking sporadically as if releasing nervous energy. Jennica silently contemplative, straddling the floor-shift. Serault almost as quiet, hearing the scream of distant jets, the closer chatter of helicopters. Watching the infrequent car, the occasional truck . . . Blinded by the sudden shrill comet of police cars nearing – shooting past, fading northwards.

Marc was strangling the wheel. 'Not us – must be the quarry.'

Serault shrugged. 'They're bound to spot it some time.'

'True . . .' Marc resettling. 'But Fernand can handle them . . .'

The road reverted to black darkness. A monotonous ribbon for the trucks to crawl up with transmissions growling, and bank down with airbrakes squelching. Exhausting the drivers and deadening the passengers long before the grey buff of coming dawn heightened the peaks. Before the peaks towered behind them, and they were entering Menton. Along streets of solitude, windless with the promise of a sweltering day. Rolling beneath windows of darkened rooms, where men gripped their sleep for respite and women gripped their men for comfort.

Serault yawning, seeing a golden glow rimming the buildings ahead of them. 'It took longer than we estimated. The sun's rising.'

Jennica looking. Rubbing her eyes, taking another weary look. 'René, it can't be. The sun's rising where it's supposed to set.'

'You're just tired,' Serault was saying as they turned onto Avenue de la Madeleine. And confronted an aura of lanterns and flares.

'Sun, hell. A roadblock.' Marc slowing, joining a line

178

idling. A second line facing, both waiting as the police searched each car. 'Too late to back up. Can't anyway, it'd only draw attention to us.'

'Ah well, we all have identification. Just act natural,' Serault said. 'And start the mixer.'

'I want to talk to Henri, too.' Marc climbed out, swearing as he engaged the mixer. Gears clashed, the truck jerking as if mortally wounded. The mixer gradually revolved gems and jewellery, money and guns, with grawling, gyrating convulsions.

Marc returned, sour. 'Leave it to Talmas to remember. Bernard had to drive the ambulance because he has the only licence.'

Jennica sighed. 'Right, the only commercial driver's licence.'

'Luckily,' Marc added, 'I'm wearing my own clothes.'

Serault eyed the headliner, not asking Marc why. He'd worried a few times during the heist when worrying had something to offer. But if Roche turned them in or Madame Ledoux ran amuck, there was nothing he could do. Not yet, not now. Not while inching forward in a stolen cement mixer churning a ton of loot. Trapped beside a girl dressed as a boy, and a driver who didn't have a licence but was luckily wearing his own clothes. Nothing he could do about any of this. Except remain in suspended animation, unquestioning, unworried.

The night grew paler, the line shorter. Their turn finally coming and Marc lurched to the roadblock. Where a bleary policeman scowled sideways at the loudly crunching mixer, down at the false nameplate, then up at Marc. 'The Degas Brothers, are you?'

'One of them.'

'Identity cards, and let's see your licence.'

Marc slowly extracted from his back pocket a wallet, bulging with cards and papers of dog-eared sizes and wine-stained edges. Coupons, permits, labels, receipts, vouchers, stamps, a youth-fare ticket for the Nice-Coni Tramway that had been destroyed in 1944. Clinically he began sorting, shuffling, sometimes dropping and having to stoop. Eventually handing a card to the policeman.

Who thrust it back. 'Degas, that isn't a driving licence.'

Marc lowered his wallet. 'Eh?'

The policeman raised his voice. 'Your driving licence.'

'Why didn't you say so?' Marc inspecting the card front and back. 'This is a crab-catching licence for Miniolta Beach. Applied for it special to please Miss Emaline. She being Emaline of the Emaline Bordella And Her All-Girl Steam Caliope Troupe, you see, and – '

'Hurry up.'

Marc nodding genially, methodically starting from scratch. The policeman stewing. 'Hurry it up.'

Marc laid down his wallet and cupped his ear.

'Sacrée soutane!' the policeman shouted. 'No wonder you can't hear. What the hell is grinding back in there, scrap iron?'

'Those little grating noises? That's the truck itself, you know how German machinery can't take the French climate.' Marc thumbing some more cards. 'Be patient, it's here somewhere. Everything is.' Humming inanely. The mixer deafening.

A bus in the other lane was discharging passengers, locals and labourers, many encumbered with bundles. Some with babies teething and bawling. Wandering over, curious. A policeman trying to corral them yelled impatiently. 'Chauvelin! Come and help inspect the bus.'

The policeman at the truck turned. 'Sir, this driver is – '

'Doubtless a clod. And doubtless the thieves are long flown, not clods in trucks heading towards Monaco. It's fruitless having to search here now, but at least this bus is pointed in a more likely direction. Pass them, Chauvelin, you're not writing traffic tickets.'

Chauvelin glaring again at Marc's vacuous face. Thumbs hooked in the shell belt hanging over his broad hips. 'If only I were . . .'

Launching ahead. Henri tagging his bumper and following before Chauvelin might object. Marc grinning smug and dirty. Jennica leaning against Serault, who felt drained with relief for having squeaked through, just as a routine check was falling into a personal confrontation. And declining into prison, if not into traction first.

The trucks sluggish up the steep grade, this final grade to Roquebrune Village. The horizon becoming defined, sky sliced from sea by a scalpel of pink. Marc reversing, easing back into the short lane to Serault's house, where Ledoux anxiously awaited, having scrubbed clean the garage and Citroën. The truck's covered chute was assembled and attached to the hopper. Marc controlling, mixer rotating, now tilting, an avalanche flowing out, and through the front door. To a bucket brigade filling the hole up around the poupée. The Vattiers bringing in the sacks and bags, then leaving to strip and repark the trucks in the excavation below. The fulgent mound raked level and covered with the tarpaulin and concrete, the brothers returning in time to help pour the last batch. Trowelling and trampling the wet ready-mix until it was flush with the rest of the basement floor . . .

The air was cream streaked with rose. Serault tottered out onto the terrace to sink at the table. Marc and Henri sprawling in nearby chairs, Kalenberg stumbling like a sleepwalker to once again lean against the railing. Jennica passing cups of well-laced coffee. All fatigued beyond conversation, listlessly watching Roquebrune awaken, and the arrival of workmen below for their Saturday half-day shift. A foreman blustering, a crescendo of engines starting, a tremoring of the terrace.

Serault enduring, bearing even the dust this morning. Tolerant with weariness and serene from the sight of Monte Carlo still smudged by smoke. A distant, dwindling silt of black and orange. His beautiful pollution. As personal an assertion as the whorls of a giant fingerprint, and he felt proud with the old price of accomplishment.

Jennica came to him, pouring more coffee. 'Satisfied?'

'Aren't you?'

'Is money, any amount of money, worth any price?'

181

Jennica with her question – her questioning – gazing out at the thin sunlight.

Serault stirring, perturbed. It was as if the night had scraped her raw, baring delicate hidden nerves and rendering her reluctant instead of ambitious. A response contrary to his expectations, since her greed had been the trigger. And yet, there'd been her disenchantment with the gala . . . I may have been figuring you wrong. But then, like most strong women, you probably don't try figuring yourself out at all . . .

His contemplations routed by a scoop-shovel biting, chewing underneath. And Ledoux storming from the house, 'She'll be the end of me,' while the hillside was shaking. 'I'll handle her. I don't know how but somehow. And after I have and we've unearthed our fortunes, I'm quitting, outright deserting that yard and that woman.'

Talmas, trailing, apologetic. 'The truth is I chickened out.'

'No, the easy way would've been to slit your own throat.'

'You proved your courage,' Jennica added. 'We all have.'

Serault, bolstering: 'And we proved to have limitations no less than yours.' Then pensive: 'There was a guard I couldn't shoot – '

'René.' Kalenberg interrupting, befuddled. 'What's that?'

Everybody staring where Kalenberg was pointing. At a glint of green and gold riding the crest of a scoop. 'An Egyptian collar of emeralds,' Serault said involuntarily, panic rising like fever in that sickening compressed moment. 'I remember it from the gala.'

The glimmer lapsing as the load was overturned into a truck. The group scouring the excavation below, alarmed by their hallucination, but dreading that it was not. Another salvo of scoop-shovels. The sun's ray's catching more winks and polish being carted away.

The fever tapering in Serault to a dazed, detached sense of inadequacy. 'I should've guessed my bedrock had seams through it,' he said in a numbed dismay. 'The weight of the jewellery plus the concrete was too much. It's all trickling down to where they're digging.'

182

'They haven't noticed.' Talmas speaking as if wringing hands.

'They will.' Acceptance of the inevitable calmed Serault, cooling his fever, purging his dismay and recriminations, even resulting in a slight rejuvenation of spirits. 'And we're fugitives.'

'If we hustle with the spades,' Marc said, 'we can still be rich fugitives.' The Vattiers fracturing a retreat for the basement. Talmas behind, keening: 'Then where'll we go?' And Ledoux following, cursing. 'Oyez! Sure as hell not back to my yard, I know.'

Jennica gamely: 'We'll shut eyes and stick a pin in the map.'

'Just one?' Serault glanced sharply at her, seeing tears gleaming on her cheeks. Of fear and failure but mainly, he sensed, of compassion and anguish for him . . . But you're learning what I've had to learn, that God never guaranteed things were supposed to work out. And what Talmas has yet to learn, that we merely can aspire to live this moment to the next, which sometimes we do well and sometimes not, but mostly we just do. And what Ledoux has forgotten: that the only bad experience is the one which kills you, inside or out. Chérie, you're learning, and you'll be fine for yourself, fine for me, though not what you were or could have been but who is. And I've managed to miscalculate you, myself, and the heist, three for the price of one. There are no answers, easy or otherwise . . .

'One pin, one map.' Serault enfolded her thighs, and Jennica stood massaging his unwashed stubbly face. 'But beware, Jennica. Our world is four-fifths water.'

And he leaned against the railing, his face a saggy mixture of defeat and requital. Watching the trucks drive down to dump Monaco's jewels into the sea as a foundation for their new summer casino.

'Merde,' Kalenberg said.